STARDOM
CAN BE
MURDER

CONNIE SHELTON

**Books
by Connie Shelton**

THE CHARLIE PARKER SERIES

*Deadly Gamble
Vacations Can Be Murder
Partnerships Can Be Murder
Small Towns Can Be Murder
Memories Can Be Murder
Honeymoons Can Be Murder
Reunions Can Be Murder
Competition Can Be Murder
Balloons Can Be Murder
Obsessions Can Be Murder
Gossip Can Be Murder
Stardom Can Be Murder*

Holidays Can Be Murder - a Christmas novella

THE SAMANTHA SWEET SERIES

*Sweet Masterpiece
Sweet's Sweets*

STARDOM
CAN BE
MURDER

Charlie Parker Mystery #12

CONNIE SHELTON

Secret Staircase Books

Stardom Can Be Murder
Published by Secret Staircase Books, an imprint of
Columbine Publishing Group
PO Box 416, Angel Fire, NM 87710

Printed and bound in the United States of America
ISBN 0615479898
ISBN-13 978-0615479897

This book is a work of fiction. Names, characters, places and
incidents are either the product of the author's imagination or are
used fictitiously. Any resemblance to actual events or locales or
persons, living or dead, is entirely coincidental. Although the author
and publisher have made every effort to ensure the accuracy and
completeness of information contained in this book we assume
no responsibility for errors, inaccuracies, omissions, or any
inconsistency herein. Any slights of people, places or organizations
are unintentional.

Book layout and design by Secret Staircase Books
Cover image © Kasia Biel
Cover background image © cekur

Also published in all e-book formats, May 2011
First trade paperback edition: May, 2011

For Dan, always my partner and my inspiration

So many people to thank for their contributions to my life and my writing career. My parents started me on the path to my creative and entrepreneurial endeavors. My daughter Stephanie is such an inspiration with her work ethic and diligence in meeting her life's goals. My son Brandon, with his free-spirited approach to life reminds me sometimes to just lighten up. My husband Dan is so supportive and never complains about the hours a writer spends locked away. My friend and editor, Susan, is there for my impossible deadlines and always comes through in a pinch. And of course there are my readers, many of whom take the time to send me encouraging notes and to so considerately spread the word by recommending my books to their friends. And, finally, to all the pets over the years who've reminded me that dinner is sometimes as important as typing one more sentence, that getting out of the chair now and then to stretch those muscles is a good thing, and that my work is way more enjoyable in their company. My heartfelt thanks to all of you!

Chapter 1

I didn't head off to the bank Friday morning with an inkling that I'd find myself at gunpoint before lunch time, but I don't suppose anyone does. The summer morning started off ordinarily enough—

Repetitive announcements blared over the airport's PA as I hugged my brother Paul for a few more seconds before letting him go to join his family. He turned to wave at our little group—older brother Ron, Ron's girlfriend Victoria, and myself—one last time before entering the rat-maze at airport security. I let out a deep breath.

"God, this was a long week," I said to Ron, finding myself in a prickly mood as we turned away and headed for the airport parking garage.

"Lucky you, getting the whole gang at your house." He grinned at the family joke.

Victoria watched us with some degree of bemusement. She's been dating Ron for a bit over six months now and is still learning our family quirks. Paul and Lorraine are okay, they're just on a different wavelength from the rest of us, and their kids . . . let's just say, they're exuberant. No, let's be truthful here—the kids run that household with a special brand of emotional blackmail and it gets really old watching the parents hop to fulfill their every little wish. Ron and I have learned over the years to just grit our teeth and pray for a quick passage of time when that group visits.

Victoria spoke up. "How about lunch later, Charlie? A long one that involves some margaritas?"

Bless the lady, she knows how to offer the right thing at the right time. Although she was dressed in her usual chic, fit for the country club style, we parted with a plan to meet at Pedro's at noon. I glanced down at my own attire, my normal jeans and a light blue summer top. I might have to class up my act if I began hanging around with Victoria. It wasn't so much that she spent a lot on clothes—she just had a way of choosing things which went together so well. You knew she never stepped out of the house without checking the mirror.

The June sky, even this early in the day, was a blue so deep it was almost painful to look at, with the temperature predicted for the high nineties and not a puff of cloud to break the heat. I watched Ron and Victoria drive off in his Mustang, then retrieved my Jeep from the airport parking garage, paid my tab, and headed west on Gibson.

Three multi-colored hot air balloons floated above the western horizon, a rare sight in the summer months. Maybe they were practicing up for the annual Balloon Fiesta, a few months away. Every year the event drew hundreds of balloonists, thousands of spectators, and several tons of cash into our economy. Thinking of cash reminded me that

I needed to stop at the bank on my way home.

I'd been longing for some time alone with Drake once my brother and his family left, but it looked like it was not to be, not yet anyway. Drake's helicopter business stayed fairly busy this spring, despite a short fire season. He'd done several photo shoots, sightseeing tours and those other miscellaneous services helicopters can perform. Now he had a customer who wanted to catch the fantastic light on the red rocks near Gallup, filming a music video at sunrise tomorrow. It would entail an overnight stay for all involved, and at over a thousand an hour for the aircraft, plus all expenses for the entire crew, it was turning into a pricey project. But they were willing. I just needed to make sure their check was going to clear before Drake turned a rotor blade for them. Nothing personal, but film companies were notoriously flaky about paying their bills.

I exited Interstate 40 at Rio Grande, passed the Sheraton and Old Town, and turned left on Central. I pulled into a neighborhood grocery, remembering that Paul's two kids had decimated our supplies of milk and bread. That little errand took no more than five minutes and I headed next for our branch of First Albuquerque Bank. Whipping into the parking lot I was pleased to see that there were only two other vehicles in front of the building.

A woman leaving the bank's ATM walked toward a small blue sedan, apparently finished with her business. Two men in an old red crew cab pickup truck parked near the door were deep in discussion. Looked like they were arguing over how to fill out a deposit slip. The one on the passenger side glanced up at me but I was walking quickly. I would easily beat them to the door.

With my choice of tellers I walked to the window of

Gina, a woman about my own age who'd waited on me many times. Today, she wore her fluffy blond hair up in a clip and had an American flag sticker attached to her standard-issue bank name tag. Her red and white sweater complimented it nicely.

"How's it going, Charlie?" she asked with a grin.

"Good, good. Just sent my houseguests off on the plane."

"Summer vacationers?"

"My middle brother. He has two kids who . . . oh, you don't want to hear it." I handed her the production company's check. "I need to be sure this will clear."

Gina started to hit some keys at her terminal but something caught her eye. She glanced up and her gaze traveled over my shoulder. "Uh-oh." Her hand slid below the counter. Her face lost about three shades of color.

I whirled around to see what had frightened her. My first coherent thought was, Why are those two guys wearing ski masks? My eyes traveled downward and caught the dull black barrel of a semi-automatic. My second thought was, Oh crap.

I turned away, avoiding the slitted eyes behind the dark blue masks.

"Hold still, Charlie," Gina whispered through her teeth. "It'll be okay."

"All right, everyone! Hands out on the counter—I want to see all hands!" The shorter man seemed jittery as he shouted orders.

I turned halfway toward them and placed both hands flat on the ledge before me. Gina's hands came up and she held them in plain sight.

I edged my eyes to the left and saw the taller of the two

men step around behind me.

"All right, tellers, all cash goes in the bags!" the short, lean guy shouted. He tossed white canvas bags over the glass divider, one to each teller. "Nothing tricky now, We're watching all of you!"

Gina and the other two female tellers opened drawers and began stuffing cash into the bags. My eyes were attracted to their motions but I knew it would be smarter to get details about the men. The jumpy one stood at the far teller cage, gun aimed at the petite Hispanic girl who was shaking like a delicate flower in a breeze. With his black jeans, black parka and dark blue ski mask there wasn't much I could distinguish about the robber. His build was wiry, and a fringe of dark hair touched his collar where the mask didn't quite cover it in back.

Movement across the room caught my eye as the bank manager emerged from her office. Shock registered momentarily on her face before the guy behind me shouted.

"Lady in a suit!" His voice came out high, with a shaky tremor. Was he younger? Or merely nervous? I couldn't see him.

The whippy guy turned on her and ordered her face down on the floor.

The manager complied, turning her face away from the rest of the room. The guy caught me looking at him.

"Make her lie down too," he shouted to the other one. He snatched the canvas bag from Gina.

I felt a nudge in my left shoulder and started to crouch down.

"No! Wait." The shorter robber cocked his head toward the door. "Somebody tripped a silent alarm. Dammit! Grab this one and let's get the hell out of here!"

The guy behind me hesitated a nanosecond.

"Now, I said! I got the money, you take her!"

A gun barrel appeared at my cheek and a hand grabbed my arm. "C'mon, lady! You're with us now," the wavering voice hissed in my ear. "Just don't cause any trouble."

My feet tangled momentarily as he shoved me toward the door. He gripped my bicep, yanking me upward and keeping me as a shield in front of both of them.

Sunlight blinded me as the tinted glass door opened. The red truck idled, facing the driveway, with its side doors open. I was shoved roughly into the back seat and the door slammed shut.

"Go, go, go!!" Hyper Guy's voice shouted at the driver. Tires chirped on pavement as the truck shot forward. The man guarding me put a big hand on my neck and pushed me down to the floor. My hip jammed into a metal toolbox. My ribs cried out. The stiff suspension bounced hard as it went off the curb. I hit the hump in the middle again and heard a horn blare about four feet from where I lay.

"Ow!" I groaned and tried to right myself again.

"Hey!" shouted Jittery Guy again. He leaned between the front seats and shook a fist at the man in the back. "Ger her blindfolded and tied up. What're you—stupid?"

Shaky Voice planted a knee between my shoulder blades and my breath exited with a whoosh. The floor of the truck smelled of grime and rust and my throat tried to close against it. My nose wasn't so lucky. An involuntary sneeze made my head jerk and I whacked my cheekbone on the uncarpeted flooring. A moan escaped me.

I struck out with both arms, screaming, with a vague hope that someone on the outside would hear me. That somehow the truck would stop and I could get away.

". . . a gag," one of the men muttered.

"I don't know. Look in the toolbox."

The sound of metal against metal as tools were jostled in the box. "Duct tape?"

Something passed behind me and I heard the sound of the tape being unwound and ripped. A silver band of it covered my mouth. I struggled and kicked as the shaky one grabbed for my arms.

"Shut her up!" the leader ordered from the front seat. "Hit the freeway," he said to the driver.

Another band of tape pulled my wrists together and circled them, then a strip of dark cloth covered my eyes. I was kicking for all I was worth when a fist to the side of my head caused tiny stars to flicker behind my blindfold. My body went limp despite my best efforts. As the stars receded, I realized that my ankles were bound now, too.

"Santa Fe?" I dimly heard the driver say to the jittery leader. "I thought we were heading for Texas." The voice was softer than Hyper Guy's, with a hint of a Spanish accent.

"Changed my mind."

"I think we made it, String," said the man in the back. "Don't hear any sirens."

"Look, everybody just shut up. We're not using names now. Little ears, you know."

Since my little ears were mostly covered and I couldn't see a damn thing, I didn't know what they thought I would do. But I huddled quietly on my side of the floor trying to appear as unconscious as I could while struggling to hear anything that might be a clue.

Chapter 2

Drake stepped out of the shower, thinking he'd heard the phone ring. He paused a moment but it had stopped. He pulled a towel off the nearby chrome and brass towel bar and scrubbed at the droplets on his face and hair. By the time he'd worked his way downward to his feet, the ringing started again. He wrapped the towel around his waist and went into the bedroom to pick it up.

"Mr. Langston?" The female voice wasn't one he recognized. Sounded like a telemarketer. He almost hung up.

"Mr. Langston, this is Gina at First Albuquerque Bank."

What did they want to sell him now?

"Can you hold for a second?"

Drake hadn't responded but she hit a button and an irritating jazzy tune played way too loudly. The phone connection clicked a couple of times and a man's voice came on.

"Drake Langston? Is your wife named Charlotte Parker?"

"Charlie. Yes, yes, what is it?" He knew the impatience in his voice wasn't going to help and he took a deep breath to control it.

"I'm Detective Dave Gonzales with APD. There was an incident here at the Central branch of the bank this morning."

"What kind of *incident*?" He chafed at the policeman's euphemism.

"Your wife was in the bank at the time, sir."

Drake couldn't wrap his head around what the detective was saying. "What's happened?"

"Can you come down here, sir? We'd like to get some information from you and it would be best to do it in person."

"What's going on here? Is Charlie all right?"

"As far as we know, sir."

"What is *that* supposed to mean. Dammit, tell me something!"

"Please come down to the bank, sir. We'll go into all of it then. It's the branch at Central and—"

"I know where it is," Drake snapped. "I'll be right there."

Grabbing the jeans and shirt he'd worn the previous day, Drake pulled them on over his damp skin and snatched a pair of deck shoes from the closet, shoving them on without benefit of socks. He raced out the front door, belatedly wondering if he'd locked it, only after he was more than a mile away.

* * *

The scene at First Albuquerque Bank sent his heart racing. Four police cars, parked at cockeyed angles, sat in the lot. Orange cones had been set up across the entrance to the drive-up windows, and at the street an officer was waving away anyone who tried to turn in. Drake pulled up to him and rolled his window down.

"Drake Langston. Detective Gonzales told me to come."

The Anglo officer, who didn't look old enough to be out of high school, hesitated a second.

"He said my wife was in the bank," Drake persisted. "That's her Jeep, over there."

"Go on through, sir." He moved one cone aside for Drake to pass.

A somewhat shakily lettered sign was taped to the glass door, informing customers that the bank would be closed temporarily. Another officer stood by to enforce that statement, until Drake identified himself once more. He pushed the lobby door open and allowed Drake past, pointing out Detective Gonzales.

The lobby bustled with activity. Uniformed police dusted surfaces with fingerprint powder. Two men in dark suits were talking with the tellers and the branch manager, off to one side. Drake tried to take it all in but the detective was walking toward him.

"Where's Charlie, and what did you mean by saying she's okay 'as far as you know'?" He willed himself to stay calm.

"Let's step in here, Mr. Langston, where it's more private." Gonzales was in his early thirties, a couple inches shorter than Drake, with caramel skin and a shaved head.

"Where is my wife?"

Gonzales touched Drake's elbow lightly. "This way," he said.

They stepped into a conference room with a whitewashed pine table, eight chairs with zia symbols carved on their backs, and a single window. When the door closed the hum of voices from the lobby disappeared.

"What's going on here?"

Gonzales sighed and scraped a hand across his shiny forehead. "There was a robbery here this morning."

"I gathered that. But . . ."

"Your wife was at the teller window when the suspects entered."

"Was Charlie hurt? Where is she?" Drake resisted the urge to scream or put his fist through the wall.

Gonzales sensed his frustration. "Well, sir, the . . . the suspects took her with them."

"What! Charlie's a hostage?" Whatever he'd thought he was going to hear, this wasn't it. A cold knot, like a ball of ice, settled in his gut.

". . . statewide alert."

"Sorry? I didn't catch all that," Drake whispered, pulling himself back into the room. The officer came into focus slowly.

"I just wanted to assure you that we've got every resource on this," Gonzales said. "FBI, city, county and state."

"What time did this happen?"

Gonzales looked at his watch. "About an hour ago."

"An hour! They could be anywhere by now!" He felt his temper flare.

The detective had the good grace to squirm a little.

"Look, I've got a helicopter. I can be airborne in—"
Drake calculated, "—in thirty minutes. Give me the
description of the vehicle."

"We can't do that."

"Why the hell not!" Drake exploded. "This is my
wife!"

The shorter man folded his arms across his chest,
revealing a holstered pistol under his jacket. "Calm down,
sir. APD and state police are already on it."

"Have they sighted the vehicle? Are they following?"

Gonzales shook his head. Then it dawned on him
what Gonzales was really saying. They had no clue where
the robbers had gone. He slumped into one of the carved
chairs.

"Sir, why don't you just—"

"Just what? Just wait patiently? Just sit around on my
hands until they've killed her?"

Gonzales backed away, his expression faltering.

"What would you be doing if it were your wife?" Drake
accused. "Losing your cool, just a little?"

The detective's tan complexion suffused with red. For
a moment he looked like he wanted to snap back, then he
sagged. "I guess so," he said simply. "I probably would be
losing it right about now."

For some reason the policeman's sympathy had a more
profound effect on Drake than the straight-up officiousness.
He felt his throat tighten and a telltale twitch began to work
on his chin. He turned his head away, took a deep breath,
blew it out.

"Okay," he said. "Look, I promise not to get in anyone's
way. But I'm not the kind of guy who can just sit around and
do nothing. Especially—" His throat clamped shut again.

"Especially when it involves the person closest to me."

The detective reached out and patted Drake on the shoulder.

"I know this has gotta hurt like hell," Gonzales offered in a soft voice. "But you have to understand that I just don't have the authority to send you out chasing them down." He glanced toward the ceiling. "I'd have my chief down on me so fast it's not even funny. Look, I can sympathize, but I got a family to feed too."

Drake gave the cop one final, hard stare then stood up. "Okay." He let the flatness in his voice convey his displeasure, but he knew it was pointless to argue further.

At the door, he paused. "Can I get someone to drive her car home for me?"

"Probably. Let's check with the Feds out front. I believe they're through processing it."

Feds. Drake walked into the lobby, realizing for the first time that half the investigators on the scene were in suits rather than uniforms. Of course, he thought. Bank robbery and kidnapping. Both were federal charges. For some reason he felt a tiny bit better.

Gonzales posed the question to the FBI senior man, a gray-haired paunchy guy with the resigned look of someone who'd hoped there wouldn't be another major case before his retirement date rolled around. He introduced himself as Cliff Kingston.

"Yeah, I don't see why not. Our guys gave the Jeep a once-over," he responded to Drake's inquiry.

Drake patted his pockets, forgetting why, then remembering that a spare key to Charlie's Jeep was on his key ring. He fumbled it, picked it up from the floor. Gina, the teller who'd called him at home stepped over, Charlie's purse in her hand.

"She dropped this. The police said they don't need it."

Drake took the purse, rubbing at the soft leather. Memories flashed through his mind—all the times Charlie had reached into that bag for something, the way she would curse when her pen or lipstick eluded her in the depths of the black lining.

"Thanks."

Gina patted his forearm and sent a sympathetic smile his way.

Gonzales wandered away and, ignoring Drake, the FBI men gathered in a knot.

Drake approached Kingston. "My wife . . . what can I—"

Kingston stepped in closer. "What's she like? Passive?"

Drake almost chuckled. Charlie, passive? Hardly.

"If she doesn't just meekly follow along, she'll probably try to save herself. Contact you. Best thing you can do is wait for a call."

Drake pictured Charlie, how she'd reacted in other bad situations. Couldn't see her whimpering in the face of danger. Kingston was right. She would try to get away or somehow contact him. But for him to wait idly by—that felt impossible.

Chapter 3

The duct tape made my face itch and one corner had caught a single hair near my temple. With each wobble of the truck it tugged at that hair with a shock that felt like a needle being drilled into my skull. I wanted to reach up and yank the hair out by its root but my bound hands, deadened into numbness, were still taped behind my back. I nudged the robber beside me and mumbled incoherently into my duct-tape gag.

"What's that?" he whispered, leaning closer.

The two men in front were talking quietly and the radio covered their words. I repeated what I'd said, which was something along the lines of, "If I ever get loose, I'm gonna kill you." My guardian spoke again, this time right near my ear.

"What you want, lady?"

The more quietly I spoke, the closer he came. I finally

let out something I hoped he'd take for a sob.

"Just a second. Be real quiet," he told me.

He peeled up a corner of the tape on my mouth, slowly, agonizingly.

"Ouch!" I whispered with a hiss.

"What'd you say back there?" The voice of the leader bellowed over the seat.

My guard sat up straighter. "Nothin', String. Didn't say nothin'." His voice wavered when he addressed the leader.

I listened as they readjusted their positions and settled down. Then I whimpered again.

Shaky Voice moved in close and a heady mixture of sweat and bad breath came at me. "If you'll stay quiet, I'll take this all the way off," he whispered.

I nodded and gritted my teeth as the remaining tape came off my mouth. No unsightly mustache for me, but I didn't care if a layer of skin was missing; I was thrilled to be able to breathe through more than my half-covered nostrils.

Judging time and distance when you're uncomfortable as hell and can't see a thing isn't easy. The truck initially made a series of jerky moves and quick turns, but had settled into a steady pace—highway pace—for quite some time now. I gradually edged at the metal toolbox with my hip until it was partway underneath the seat, giving me a tad more space on the floor. With that little luxury came the ability to shift my weight off my shoulder and arm and let some blood flow to my numb hand. The kerchief had slipped off my eyes and my guard didn't replace it.

How much time had passed, I couldn't begin to guess. It might have been fifteen minutes or an hour. When I sensed slight variations in speed, I imagined that we might be approaching an exit, a town . . . I couldn't tell. I strained to make out words in the scant exchanges of conversation between the men but phrases like "up ahead" "pretty soon" and "over there" didn't add a lot to my understanding.

The truck abruptly took a left turn and nearly went up on two wheels. It slithered sickeningly, a graveled surface spitting rocks that felt like they were hitting my ribs through the hot metal flooring. My eyes went wide and a glance at my guard showed his doing the same.

The radio music died abruptly. "Easy, stupid!"

I heard a smack, like the guy in charge had given the driver a slap upside the head.

"Sorry, String." The truck slowed considerably and we bumped over a rutted track with a loping motion. It took every bit of my self control to keep my stomach from hurling.

Eventually, the vehicle yanked to a stop, sending me slamming against the back of the driver's seat. Both front doors opened and the truck swayed as the two men exited. I struggled to my knees, catching a view of sandy high-desert terrain dotted with piñon and short juniper trees. The location could be just about anywhere along the Rio Grande corridor within a hundred-fifty miles of Albuquerque in any direction. Something about the configuration of nearby mountains made me think we might be near Santa Fe.

". . . do you think she went?" The voice of the driver wafted my way on the hot breeze.

We'd stopped in front of a small building, maybe a ranch house. Weathered wood siding had once been painted white, but that was a long time ago. The graying boards clung haphazardly, badly in need of repair. Gray asphalt shingles curled on the roof and the windows were hung with curtains—one red, one blue—faded to chalky hints of their true colors. The place appeared abandoned.

The other man said something but his words didn't carry to me. He was skeletally thin, not very tall, with greasy black hair combed straight back from his low forehead and at least a day's growth of heavy dark beard. His shoulders were straight, his chest thrust forward, his stance reminding me of a bantam rooster. He wore black jeans and a black polyester shirt and chewed at the earpiece of a pair of black wraparound sunglasses, which he held with a nervous sort of energy that made me want to stay clear of him. This was the leader, the one who'd shouted the orders inside the bank. He walked up to the house and pounded on the door. No response.

The driver spoke again. "What you want to do, String?" Slight Spanish accent, a little younger than the other guy, dressed in jeans and a T-shirt with a biker gang logo on it. Multi-colored tattoos started at his wrists and disappeared beneath his sleeves.

The one called String started to turn back toward the truck.

"Get down!" My guard's voice was insistent. "You don't want String to see you up like that."

"There's nobody out there to see me. I need to sit up. Lying down is making me carsick." I shifted, not waiting for permission.

He hesitated and I got my first real look at him. Early twenties, a pretty well-established beer belly, that soft pudgy look of a well-fed kid.

"What's your name?" I asked, settling my butt onto the

hard metal floor. On the seat, near my face, lay a heap of canvas bags—the money from the bank.

"Billy. But the guys call me Domino." He shrugged and glanced nervously out the window. It must have seemed safe to keep talking. "Cause I work at a pizza place."

"Ah." I tried to give as winning a smile as a girl can give when she's got duct-tape goo on her face and sweat forming on clothing that's been rumpled on the floor of a dirty old pickup. "Well, you seem a lot nicer than the others."

He shrugged again then his eyes went wider. "Shh!" He shifted in his seat and loosely stuck the used strip of duct back over my mouth. "Don't get me in trouble."

I wanted to tell him they were already in way more trouble than he was ready for. But that wouldn't have earned me any brownie points at the moment.

From my lowly vantage point I could barely see the heads and shoulders of the other two but it was clear that some sort of argument was in progress. Muted words flew, hands and fingers gestured.

"Get back down! Here they come," Billy whispered.

I rolled to one hip again, the whole bound-limbs thing really hampering any movement at all. It wasn't as if I was going to leap out and overpower anyone.

"I can't *believe* that bitch!" String said as he planted himself in the front passenger seat and slammed the door. "Just have the car here. It's all I asked."

The driver climbed in slowly, not commenting.

Billy sat so still I was positive he was holding his breath.

"So, where else would she be?" the driver finally asked.

"Well, she better be at Sissy's. She ain't—she's dead meat."

His voice was low and dangerous and he sounded like he meant it. I kept my eyes firmly on the edge of the back seat. This guy, String, clearly wasn't somebody to mess with.

"So—go, Mole! Dammit!"

The driver cranked the engine back to life and hit the gas. I bit the side of my mouth as he hit the swale at the edge of the driveway again. Back on the bumpy gravel road he didn't ease off at all. My body was going to be *so* bruised by tomorrow. If there was a tomorrow. I concentrated on taking an inventory of the things under the truck's backseat—I couldn't let myself dwell on the other possibility.

At least an hour must have passed, during which we'd gotten back onto a paved highway, exited again, off onto a sandy road—this I figured out when the truck swerved, tires grabbing with that almost-stuck feeling—followed by a slow cruise down a narrow lane and into another driveway.

"All right," String said. " 'Bout damn time."

My sentiments exactly. My stomach was doing flip-flops and if I'd had a meal recently it would have been all over Billy's shoes. My head felt like a tennis ball in a Federer match.

Billy must have gotten some sense of my plight because as soon as the truck came to a halt he helped me get to my knees and then opened his side door.

String shot him a sharp look over his shoulder.

"She's gettin' sick, boss. I just gotta give her a little air. She can't go nowhere."

String clearly didn't care but he didn't say anything. He and Mole got out and walked toward the tan stucco house where we were parked. Beside the truck sat a silver sedan that had oxidized to a dull gray. A young woman in a tight purple tank top came onto the small front porch as they approached and String let out with a tirade about her being there, about messing up the plan.

She flipped her dark hair over her shoulder and sassed back with a sort of you're-not-the-boss-of-me attitude and turned her back on him. He grabbed her arm and spun her around, backhanding her across the mouth. Her dark eyes went wide and a trickle of blood ran down her chin. She kept quiet when he shoved her toward the house.

An older woman appeared briefly at the door—blond hair, blowsy features, a tad overweight—but she quickly ducked out of sight when she saw the men. Neither of the women glanced toward the truck. I might have found an ally between them, but it wasn't looking hopeful.

I lifted my shoulder and wiped my mouth against it until the duct tape came off. "What are they going to do with me?" I whispered to Billy.

Again, the shrug. Didn't this guy know one single thing? If I'd had an available leg I would have kicked him in the shins.

"Look, this is killing me. Find out if my hands can be tied in front of me. My shoulder feels like it's getting dislocated. And can I at least sit up?"

He did have the good grace to look like he was sorry. "I'll ask," he said in that same shaky voice.

Mole, the driver, came back and started the truck again. Billy posed my requests to him as he steered the truck toward a large barn behind the house. Mole took a full two minutes to consider. I got the feeling that dealing with a woman who was bound and gagged was not a new situation for him. An icy chill slid over my arms as he stared at me in the mirror.

"Do it," he said, finally.

He jerked the truck to a stop beside a ten-year-old Jeep Cherokee inside the barn and held one of the guns on me as Billy worked on my duct tape. Dang. If he'd left us alone I'd have been real tempted to grab that tire iron I'd spotted under the seat and whack Billy the minute my arms were free. But no such luck. Mole, with his hard eyes and cruel mouth and those creepy tattoos, watched as Billy cut off the old tape and rebound my wrists, this time to the front of me. I braced them as far apart as I could, subtly, but he was pretty vigorous with the tape.

"Are we leaving her here, Mole? In the truck?"

Again, that chilling stare. "No, Domino. She's going with us."

My stomach lurched again.

"Cut her feet loose. I don't want to carry her to the car," Mole said.

It was amazing how grateful I felt for that one small favor.

My feet stumbled, touching the ground for the first time in hours. I gingerly put my weight on them and took a few practice steps; Mole's gun stayed on me the whole time. I glanced at my wrist, forgetting that I'd left my watch at home this morning.

"Domino, grab the bags," Mole ordered. "You, lady, over to the car."

Billy pulled the three canvas bags from the back seat of the truck and walked behind me, near Mole, doing his best to look as tough as the other man but not really pulling it off. We stopped just outside the barn where String waited and he shoved the tall door closed. His pistol was jammed into the waistband of his black jeans, handy at a moment's notice. I avoided staring at it.

On the porch, the girlfriend in the purple top waited. Apparently once String's anger dissipated they'd patched things up enough that she wanted to say goodbye. For all I knew, maybe she planned on coming along as part of the entourage. She gave me a long stare as we passed. Oh, no, don't put me in the middle of some jealous-girlfriend thing, I thought. I held up my bound hands, just to demonstrate that my being here was not my idea.

All at once she grinned hugely. "Cristina Cross! Ohmygod, you're Cristina Cross!"

Uh . . . no. I had no clue what she was talking about. String strode over to her and gripped her arm, leading her into the house, while Billy threw the money bags into the open trunk of the car and Mole nudged me toward the back seat with the muzzle of the gun. Back seat beats trunk any day, so I complied.

"Down on the floor again!" he ordered.

Oh, crap. But I went, hoping against hope that he wouldn't remember to tape my ankles again. I got lucky for the moment; he slammed the door and Billy took up his position again as my guard. Mole started the car, which purred like a silken cello compared to the old truck.

The front passenger side door stood open, waiting for String. The sun blasted full-force on the car and sweat trickled from my hairline. Apparently, it had no air conditioning. Ten minutes must have passed, during which no one in the vehicle spoke. I could tell that Mole was getting restless.

Two muffled shots sounded, somewhere out of sight.

Mole tensed, and I felt a jolt of adrenaline race through me. A minute later String dashed out of the house and jumped into his seat. He plopped a plastic grocery bag on the center console while he slammed his door.

"Lunch," he announced. "I had Melinda make us a sandwich."

The car took off, slithering through the soft spots in the sandy road, heading back toward the highway. My mind raced with the knowledge of what I'd heard back there. Two women in that house. Two shots. No more witnesses.

Billy was a little wide-eyed but the other men acted like nothing had happened. String pulled the plastic bag onto his lap and rummaged through it. He retrieved sandwiches and passed one to each of the men. The car filled with the scent of peanut butter as Billy bit into his.

"Here," String said. "Melinda sent one for the lady, too."

The plastic bag crinkled as he handed another sandwich to the back seat. Billy took it and placed it in my bound hands. I wasn't exactly hungry, considering, but I managed a few bites.

Mole turned to their leader. "So, what was that all about?" he asked.

"On the porch there?"

"Yeah."

"She swears the lady is some television star. One of them daytime shows, the soaps, I guess. Does movies too." String leaned over the seat and stared at me, still crouched on the floor. "Your name Cristina Cross?"

I felt my mouth gape open.

He didn't wait for an answer. "Don't you see?" he said

to Mole. "This is better than the whole bank thing. We got something valuable now. We can get a huge ransom for a movie star."

Chapter 4

Oliver Wendell Trask reached into his jeans pocket. He felt the gaze of the motel clerk on his hands as he extracted two twenties from the wallet that was attached to his belt loop by a chain, and slid them across the worn Formica counter.

" 'Nother two seventy-five," the man monotoned. "Gotta send the governor his share."

Oliver carefully pulled out three more singles. He watched as the chubby, balding man in grimy blue work pants and a sagging sleeveless undershirt cracked open a paper roll of quarters and emptied them into a cardboard tray in the drawer. He held out his hand to receive one of the shiny disks and noticed rims of black encrusted around each of the clerk's fingernails. Sadie Trask might not have been much in the mothering department but she'd drilled the concept of clean fingernails into Ollie for most of their fourteen years together. He held his palm a couple of inches below the other man's fingers so he'd drop the coin without their hands touching.

The clerk turned to a pegboard on the side wall of his cubicle, displaying copious armpit hair as he reached for a key.

"Number 10, far end of the parking lot. Vending machines're right here outside the office, checkout time's eleven in the morning." His eyes traveled toward the two large plate glass windows at the front of the barren ten-foot-square lobby. Ollie knew he was looking for the car, no doubt hoping to catch a peek at whatever female Ollie had brought with him, but he'd parked on the windowless side of the building. And there was no female with him.

"Lucky we had a vacancy this early in the day."

"Yeah, guess so." He shuffled slightly, unsure how much chit-chat was required in this situation. "Been driving all night. Gotta get me some sleep."

"Yeah."

He hated the way the clerk looked at him, critical of his youth and inexperience, or like he knew something was up. Ollie was far too wired to look sleepy right now. He palmed the old fashioned room key with its blue plastic tag and walked out into the blazing Texas sun. He felt the clerk's stare as he walked around the side of the building.

The Shady Rest Motel was one of those places that had probably enjoyed a steady clientele of family guests at some point in its life. Somewhere around 1966 the Interstate highway had bypassed old Texas 435 and by the '70s and '80s the Holiday Inns and Ramadas had siphoned off the family traffic. The Shady Rest would have become an out-of-the-way place for businessmen from outlying towns to spend their lunch hours with someone else's wife or the occasional trucker who happened to know the place was here and didn't have an expense account to cover something better.

Oliver climbed behind the wheel of the rusted out white '79 Pontiac and, out of habit, held his breath while the starter ground repeatedly until she finally caught. He tapped the gas pedal a couple of times and black smoke woofed out the tailpipe.

"Piece a shit," he muttered.

The car coughed.

"*Nice* piece a shit." He humored the heap that was older than he was. Hey, even though it was nearly as old as his mother, it hadn't cost him anything and once it got purring along the highway it didn't cause much trouble.

It took a couple of minutes before he was confident enough to put the car in gear, but she stayed running and he eased her out of the open dirt lot beside the motel office and onto the badly paved parking area. Cruising to the far end of the L-shaped building, he caught the smarmy clerk backing away from the windows as he coasted the car into the slot outside number 10.

Some kind of dusty tree hung over the end of the building here, but its wind-bent branches didn't put out much shade. Random hollyhock plants grew in a hit-and-miss fashion across the front of the plain cinderblock units, flowers that had probably been planted twenty years ago by some manager's wife who thought a little cheerfulness would bring more guests. Now they'd gone to seed so many times that they came up wherever they felt like it, including the cracks in the parking lot and one that seemingly grew out of the cinderblock building itself and angled partway across the door to number 10. Ollie gave it a shove with his battered duffle bag while he slid the key into the lock in the flimsy door handle. Dried up seed pods scattered into the twelve-inch strip of dirt that passed for a flower bed.

Inside the gloomy room he tossed his bag onto the sagging double bed. A wood laminate nightstand with chipped corners and cigarette burns held a teardrop-shaped orange ceramic lamp, which he switched on. Its puny yellow light revealed a dresser of the same era but not from the same set, with a thirteen inch television set crudely bolted to its top. Orange shag carpet, caked now into a mass of flattened strings, and a bedspread in faded shades of orange and brown indicated that someone had once attempted a decorating theme.

Ollie wasn't sure what that theme might be exactly, but it was nicer than the efficiency apartment he'd just been evicted from so he closed the door and plopped down on the squishy mattress. He kicked off his work boots and stretched, resting his head on his arms. A contented sigh escaped.

His eyes opened a few minutes later and he realized he'd drifted off to sleep, his thoughts meandering around the fact that he'd walked off the latest in a series of loser jobs, this time busting tires for a buck over minimum wage. Better than getting splattered with grease at the donut shop, dishwashing at that one diner, or the whole series of other crappy gigs that had barely kept him in rent money these past four years. At least now he had the prospect of some real cash.

Shit, he thought, sitting up abruptly. The schedule. He glanced at the digital clock on the nightstand. 12:03. The guys could be rolling in any minute.

He swung his legs over the edge of the bed and scrubbed at the sides of his sandy blond hair with both hands. His head felt fuzzy.

The bathroom glared stark white at him when he switched on the light. A chipped enamel tub sat across one end of the tiny room, matching sink directly ahead. The convenience he was looking for was jammed between the other two. He raised the seat, unzipped and peed long and luxuriously into the clear water, not bothering to remove the paper band someone had strapped across the seat.

Rearranging himself comfortably afterward, he wished he *had* brought a woman to the motel. Rena Lynn. The others could be arriving any time now, but she and Ollie were usually quick about it. He shifted the front of his jeans again, trying to make the image of her shimmering blond hair and firm seventeen-year-old breasts go away but it didn't help. He turned on the cold water tap at the sink.

The water was lukewarm, reminding him that there weren't deep, cold reserves of water here, like there were in New Mexico. He let it run for five or six minutes and the lukewarm stream eventually turned coolish. He splashed his face with it, dispersing the sleep-fuzzed lint balls in his brain and taking his libido one step further away from Rena Lynn.

Another glance at the clock told him it was now 12:13. He walked to the front window and held back one orange and brown drape. The Pontiac was the only vehicle in the lot. Lucky to have a vacancy this early in the day. What a slimeball that guy was, thought Ollie. He spotted the vending machines by the office and suddenly wanted a cold Coke worse than he'd wanted anything in a long time. His mouth felt like the inside of his boot, and swishing the tepid water around his fuzzy-feeling teeth hadn't helped a bit.

He dug his hand into his front pocket and came up with the one quarter the clerk had given him in change. That wouldn't be enough for a vending machine Coke, he knew, and he was all out of small bills. The other pocket yielded the car keys and his four-inch pocket knife. No coins. He really didn't want to go back and ask the creepy manager for change.

Besides, what if the other guys called? He again cursed the fact that String hadn't gotten him a cell phone. He tried to remember the plan. Were they coming directly here or would they call first? After their pre-dawn meeting in Tucumcari, they should have had plenty of time to drive to Albuquerque, do the job and get here. What if something had gone wrong? He tried to remember—was he supposed to leave after awhile, go after them? They'd never talked about the plan not working, what to do if they failed. But it was going to work. Ollie focused on that.

He stretched out on the bed again but the idea of getting a cold drink from the machines wouldn't leave him alone. Finally, he shoved his boots back on, grabbed the plastic ice bucket from the dresser top and stalked out the door. In the office the manager was nowhere to be seen. Ollie decided, what the hell. He leaned over the counter and pulled open the drawer where he'd seen the man empty the new roll of quarters. In one smooth move, he grabbed a handful of them, pushed the drawer closed, and jammed the change into his front jeans pocket before strolling out to the set of vending machines.

Five minutes later he'd settled back in the room with a frigid can of Coke, a bucketful of ice, and two packs of peanut butter crackers. He switched on the TV set and flipped through channels until he came upon something mildly pornographic. But it only served to remind him of Rena Lynn. He switched the set off, frustrated.

Soon, he promised himself. He stretched out on the bed again and envisioned the future. With his share of the money, which ought to be at least a hundred thou, he'd buy her a house, a really nice one with a front porch and white walls inside and beige carpet, wall-to-wall. And it'd be big, even bigger than a double-wide. It should have at least two bedrooms, and knowing Rena Lynn's love of kids better make that three.

And he'd buy himself a new car, a red Corvette. They could put the top down and take long drives and her silky blond hair would fly in the wind. He could get that puppy up to 120, he'd bet, on some of these straight, endless Texas farm roads. Maybe Rena Lynn'd have so much fun riding in the new car that she'd forget about having kids and it could be just the two of them, riding around and living the carefree life.

The sound of a vehicle outside popped his future-bubble, sending him to the door so fast that little black dots swam before his eyes. He rubbed at them with his left hand while his right reached for the knob.

Nothing.

The red truck he expected to see was nowhere in sight. Instead, a battered blue Chevy Nova was just completing a loop through the parking lot and preparing to swing back out onto the highway. Oliver's heart slowed back down again.

Course he wasn't exactly sure what vehicle to be watching for, he reasoned. Yeah, they'd been driving the truck first thing this morning, but knowing String he'd have been smart enough to trade that out for something else by now. What if they came to the motel and he didn't see them?

He closed the door and opened the orange and brown drapes as wide as they'd go, which wasn't all the way, due to a bent place in the curtain rod, but it was enough that he could sit in the room's one chair and stare out and pretty much cover the parking lot. Besides, they knew his vehicle. The old Pontiac belonged to String and it had New Mexico plates. So they'd find him, no matter what they were driving. He relaxed into the chair, his Coke in hand as he polished off one of the packs of crackers.

His stomach growled at the addition of food. Damn crackers, he thought. What he really wanted was a nice, big cheeseburger with some fries and a chocolate shake. He tried to remember whether he'd seen any food places near the motel. Couldn't think of any. The McDonald's and Burger Kings were near the Interstate next to the decent motels. Too far to walk and he didn't dare take off in the car. If the guys came to the motel and didn't see any sign of him they'd think he'd chickened out and they'd keep his share of the money.

He downed the other pack of crackers and stood up to dig into his pockets for more change. He was down to two quarters, not enough for another purchase from the machines. Everything cost seventy-five cents out there. The rooms might go for yesterday's prices but everything else here was top-dollar. He glanced toward the office and could see the chubby clerk moving around inside the tiny space. At least he'd put a shirt on.

"Well, shit," Ollie grumbled. No more free quarters and he couldn't chance it that the guy had already discovered the missing ones. He flopped back into the chair and stared, heavy-lidded, at the driveway.

When he opened his eyes again the sun was well past mid-point in the sky. His neck had a terrible crick in it and one foot had fallen asleep. His stomach growled and he looked at the clock again.

A prickle of alarm raced up his spine. It was way too late. Something was wrong.

He decided to do the one thing he'd been told never to do—call String on his cell phone.

He rolled his aching neck in a big arc as he punched numbers into the bedside telephone. A familiar voice responded on the second ring.

"Yeah?" The voice was made of sandpaper with oil spread on top—at once slick and quietly threatening. Ollie's private parts never failed to shrink just a little when that voice addressed him.

"String? Where are you guys?" His voice quivered just a little, and he knew String picked up on it.

"Hey, Kid. Where you at?"

"Well, I'm at the motel in Texas, just like we planned. But where are you guys? Did everything go okay?"

"Listen, Kid, there's been a little change of plans."

"What . . . what kind of change?"

Oliver realized he was speaking to a dead phone.

Chapter 5

My head spun. Ransom? I was pretty sure two women were already dead and now these guys thought I could be worth big money to them. I wanted to tell them that they had the wrong person, but then where would I be?—useless and knowing too much—just like Melinda and the other one.

A cell phone rang and String grabbed his shirt pocket, bringing the phone out and opening it in one swift move. He addressed the caller as Kid, sent a couple of terse sentences his way and clicked the phone shut. A change of plans.

I really didn't want to be someone's change of plans. I wanted to go home—now. I wanted to be lunching in a restaurant with Victoria, then go home and hold my husband and spend the evening having great sex. If I couldn't have my dream scenario, I'd even agree to having Paul and Lorraine and their kids back for a longer visit. Well, maybe.

How did my simple trip to the bank turn into a ride with three strange and dangerous men who were now discussing me as if I were their lottery ticket?

The car's mushy suspension hit bottom as Mole roared over a dip and onto paved highway. My tailbone cracked against the flooring and I yelped in pain.

"Boss," said Billy. "Maybe we better be treating her nicer than this."

String turned in his seat and glared down at me.

"I mean, her being somebody important and all . . ." Billy's voice had gone shaky again.

String's wheels were turning, I could tell. It wasn't especially surprising that polite gestures didn't occur naturally to him. I held my breath, half-wishing that Billy hadn't mentioned me. Being invisible was preferable at this point.

A slimy grin spread across String's dark features, revealing pointy teeth and a fair amount of plaque. Not exactly a friendly smile. His eyes were hard, calculating. I *really* wanted to be invisible now.

"Let her sit on the seat," he told Billy.

I glanced over at my guard. He hustled to follow String's instructions. While the dark-haired boss turned to watch the road, Billy reached down and put a hand under my arm. With the small boost, I was able to get my feet under me and hike myself onto the back seat, behind the driver.

"Thanks," I mouthed toward Billy. He raised one corner of his mouth in a tiny smile.

"Buckle her up," String ordered.

He cared?

"We can't afford to get stopped for a stupid seat-belt

ticket." He turned the radio up again and a throbbing rap tune filled the car.

Now that we were riding in a completely different vehicle from the one seen at the bank, the gang seemed to relax a little. Billy leaned against the window beside him and I caught him nodding off a couple of times. Mole tapped his index fingers on the steering wheel as if he were hitting it with drum sticks, in time with the music. String edged lower in his seat, his head reclining against the headrest. A little post-murder nap?

I tried to concentrate on what to do about my situation. Roaring down the highway at seventy miles an hour, my hands bound with duct tape, didn't seem like a feasible time to make a break for it. All three of the men had guns, and although Billy seemed the least likely to use his, I couldn't be sure of anything. They'd kept me tightly guarded every single minute I was outside the car.

Who was this actress with whom they had me confused? Cristina Cross. I'd heard the name but couldn't remember any of her roles. I knew I should have watched more daytime TV, darnit.

I ran through dimly remembered images of faces I might have seen in my limited exposure to *People* magazine, women with long auburn hair and maybe with my same green eyes, but that narrowed the possibilities to only a hundred or so. I couldn't seem to focus very well. Luckily, the gang didn't know much about her either. At least I didn't have to replicate a voice or mannerisms that I knew nothing about.

We only spent a short time on the Interstate before String instructed Mole to take an exit. I'd seen no mileage signs, no nice clear list of upcoming cities, so I only had the vaguest notion of our location. Somewhere north of Santa Fe, I thought. Obviously, String wanted us away from the major routes where police cars and other drivers might get a look at us.

I felt so drowsy. My lips were burning, chapped from the dry air and the fact that the duct tape gag had ripped off any shred of the lipstick I'd put on at some point, about a lifetime ago. These are the times when a woman really misses her purse. All those little conveniences—lip balm, hairbrush, cell phone, pistol. I'd last seen my bag lying on the floor of the bank. I hoped the police had called Drake. I wanted him to come get me. Darn—now my eyes were burning too. I gave in to the lethargy and let my body slump into the corner.

Chapter 6

Ollie Trask dropped the dead receiver back into its cradle, his mind numb. String and the other guys wouldn't just go off and leave him. There'd been the plan. They'd worked it all out. Two guys into the bank, quick and easy. One guy driving the truck. One guy, him, getting the safe house secured. And here he was, in the safe house, a place no one would ever think to look for them and he'd staked it out to be sure no cops came around. So, okay, it wasn't exactly a house, this fourth-rate motel, but it was about as invisible as you could get. So, maybe he'd dozed off a couple of times. He was still pretty sure no cops had checked out the place yet.

How could they just leave him here? He drummed his fingers on the cheap nightstand. His aunt Sissy, mother of String's girlfriend, was the one who'd gotten Ollie in with the gang. Surely String didn't want to piss her off by excluding Ollie? He chewed at the ends of his mustache as he thought about it.

The money.

They didn't want to split the money four ways.

A hot, blind rage boiled up inside Oliver Wendell Trask. Nobody was doing him out of his share, not that easy. He flung the half-empty Coke can against the cinderblock wall, missing the TV set by inches. The drink still had enough fizz in it to explode on impact, leaving sticky brown fingers running down the wall, forming a puddle on the orange carpet.

Ollie spun around, breath hissing forcefully through his teeth, fists clenched into white-knuckled balls. Dammit! Damn it all to hell anyway! He snatched his worn duffle off the bed. He'd go after those guys. No way were they going to treat him like the dumbass high school dropout they thought he was. No way would Sissy stand for them dissing her nephew. Not Ollie Trask. No sir.

He yanked the car keys from his jeans pocket, tossed the duffle into the back seat, and nearly caught his foot in the door as he climbed in and slammed it. Jamming the key into the ignition he shoved the gas pedal to the floor and cranked. The old Pontiac groaned like a bear waking up from hibernation but she didn't start. Flooded. He cursed.

Ollie took a deep breath and forced himself to calm down. Tricky old tub wasn't going anywhere unless he coaxed her along—he knew that. He rested his forehead against the steering wheel and counted to twenty.

A gentle foot on the gas pedal and a cautious twist of the key. The car groaned again but by the third deep moan, the ignition kicked to life and the reassuring puff of black smoke shot from her tailpipe. Ollie eased the gas pedal steadily down until the engine smoothed out.

"*Nice* piece a shit," he crooned, patting her dashboard

gently. Inside, his guts were still churning. He shifted into reverse, praying that the old beast wouldn't desert him now. He'd been deserted enough for one day.

The engine held and the car jerked away from the tacky cinderblock motel building. Ollie realized, after he'd shifted back into Drive, that he'd left the door to the room standing open. Forget it. He floored the pedal and squealed the tires as he whipped the old boat toward the highway. The slimy clerk stood in the office doorway, staring at the Pontiac, his mouth working. Well, good riddance to him!

Twenty minutes later Ollie used his last fifteen dollars to get a burger from a drive-thru place and add gas to the tank. He wished he had enough to stop somewhere and get one of those prepaid cell phones; it would have made things easier right now but it was the story of his life—always short on money. That was another thing that twisted at Ollie's guts—he'd spent his own cash to get this rattletrap from Tucumcari to Texas and now he was having to chase down the rest of the gang to get his rightful share. He coaxed the Pontiac into gear and rolled away from the gas pumps, perching his burger at the top of the steering wheel to unwrap it. His teeth snatched a generous bite as he roared onto the ramp to Interstate 40.

The plan, after meeting up at the motel in Texas, was to abandon the truck somewhere and then take the Pontiac as their getaway vehicle. None of the guys had told Ollie where they would ultimately end up, but his impression was that they would divide the loot and spread out. Harder for the cops to catch up with them that way. Ollie liked that idea because he was the one guy who hadn't been at the bank.

It'd be pretty hard for some cop to pin the robbery on *him*.

So, he debated as he pushed the Pontiac to its limits—crossing the New Mexico line and heading toward Albuquerque—since they didn't come for him, where *did* they go?

He spent about fifty miles thinking about it before it hit him that String would head for Melinda's place. He'd probably already told her that he was taking her car and leaving the truck with her. Melinda was just dumb enough to take that as a compliment, the fact that her boyfriend would let her drive his truck around.

Ollie pulled off the interstate at Santa Rosa and found a pay phone at a truck stop. He got the operator to place the collect call to Melinda's house but the voice that answered wasn't hers.

At the operator's query about accepting the call, the girl said, "Mel's gone to her mom's. Prob'ly be back later."

The operator offered to call another number for him but Ollie declined. He'd gotten the information he wanted. He'd rather go to Sissy's anyway. He could bum some money from his aunt if the guys weren't there and she would probably send him off with something more to eat.

He'd never been quite clear on how, exactly, Sissy was related. She wasn't his mother's sister, he knew that. Someplace back in the fuzzy reaches of time, he had the impression that she'd been the sister of one of his mother's long-gone boyfriends. Didn't really matter. Sissy was always nice to him as a kid.

Sissy lived north of Santa Fe, out on some acreage at the far ass-end of a dirt road that didn't go anywhere important. Ollie climbed back into the car. His gas gauge was registering less than half a tank—quite a bit less—and he had no cash left. At the very least String could have given him one of those prepaid credit cards but no—he hadn't even been polite enough to do that. He forced himself to calm down. Being angry and ready to lash out wasn't going to get him what he wanted here. He glanced around the truck stop, spotting his mark.

"Ma'am?" he said, approaching a middle-aged woman who'd just started pumping gas into her mid-sized sedan. She wore a flowered dress with a lace collar that screamed church-lady. "I'm wondering if you might help me out, ma'am? I have to get to El Paso by this afternoon, cause my baby sister is having an operation." He sniffed. "They aren't sure she'll make it."

He glanced at the Pontiac, which he'd left near the pumps on the next island over. "My car's nearly out of gas and"—he patted his pockets—"I'm all out of cash. Is there any way you could top off my tank for me?"

She finished her own fill-up and looked at him, torn between doing the polite thing and the smart thing. He could practically read the thoughts racing through her head. At least he wasn't asking for cash. And he really did look broken up about his little sister. He sniffled again and thought of the time his dog had been hit by a car, bringing up just enough of a sad memory that his eyes brimmed.

"Sure, son. Pull over to this pump and we'll just add it to my purchase."

Ollie had hoped for cash but hey, at least this would give him plenty of gas to get where he needed to go. He coaxed the Pontiac to life, noticing that the woman flinched at the racket it made, but happy that the old tub started on the first try.

He took the gas hose from her and pumped his tank

full, then thanked her profusely. She stood with one hand
on the driver's door of her car, looking ready to lock herself
inside. Don't overdo it, dude, he reminded himself.

Minutes later he was on the Interstate again, stayed there
until he came to the turnoff for Las Vegas. Sissy's place was
somewhere between Vegas and Santa Fe. He never could
figure out why New Mexico had a Las Vegas, when there
was the famous one in Nevada, but vaguely remembered a
history teacher in middle school saying this one had been
there for a couple hundred years before the famous one was
started. Something about the railroads or the Santa Fe Trail
or something . . . he never kept track of that kind of stuff.

It took another couple of hours but Ollie relaxed into
the drive. At least he didn't have to worry about running
out of gas out here in the middle of nowhere. He came to
Interstate 25, went west and recognized the exit for Sissy's
just in the nick of time. He slammed on the brakes and left
tread marks as he wheeled onto the narrow frontage road.
A few more turns and he'd come to her little sandy lane.
Several sets of tracks showed in the powder-dry dirt; maybe
the rest of them were here now, waiting and laying low from
the law. At least they wouldn't get past him on this road
without him seeing them. He began to breathe easier.

Even though Sissy's house was out in the middle of
nothing, Ollie had always liked it. Tan stucco, white trim
which kind of needed a touchup, a huge weathered barn
where he remembered playing a few times as a kid, even a
couple of big elm trees. Other than that, the land around
here was plain old tan earth dotted with a lot of piñon and
juniper trees. They were too short for much climbing, even
for a kid, and you had to be careful this time of year because

the heat brought out the rattlesnakes.

He cruised up the dirt track that made a loop which Sissy called the driveway. Not another car in sight. Weird. Melinda's car should have been here. Or Sissy's Jeep. Or the red truck. He brought the clattery Pontiac to a stop but no one came out. Sissy always greeted him at the porch.

Maybe she and Melinda had gone off on some kind of girly shopping trip to the city.

Maybe the gang had never made contact with Melinda.

Maybe Ollie's butt was about to be in a sling because they expected him to stay at that motel in Texas. His gut clenched a little at the thought of String's wrath.

But no, String'd said that there was a change of plans. And they sure couldn't get mad at him because he was trying to find out what the new plan was, right?

He slowly turned off the ignition. String would do any damn thing he wanted, and taking it out on Ollie would fit right in with his normal way of handling things. He sat there a minute, debating what to do next, when he noticed that Sissy's front door wasn't completely closed. Now that just wasn't right.

Ollie got out of the car and walked toward the small porch. The door was standing open several inches and flies were buzzing around. Sissy wasn't a picky housekeeper but she hated flies. On a day like this, that door would be closed.

"Sissy!" he called out.

Not a sound.

"Sissy! You home?" He didn't even hear a radio or TV set. He fidgeted from one foot to the other. Maybe when the girls went shopping they'd forgotten to be sure the door latched. He walked up to it and tapped lightly, sending it swinging open.

When he spotted the bodies he suddenly understood. Then he ran for the nearest patch of cactus and retched.

Chapter 7

Feeling dazed, Drake walked into the empty house. His footsteps echoed through the rooms where the rumpled linens on the guest bed reminded him of their recent company and how badly he and Charlie wanted a little time to themselves now. He bundled up the sheets and tossed them beside the washer, listening for the phone.

In his office he called Charlie's brother, Ron, to let him know about the morning's events. Having a private investigator in the family gave them a slight edge, or he hoped it would. Drake heard horns in the background.

"Sorry, I shouldn't have sprung this on you while you're in the car. Call me back when you get to a safe spot," he said.

Remembering that he had a customer depending on him, he looked up the number and called the music video producer to let them know he would have to put their filming job on hold. The woman grumbled but finally agreed to reschedule when she heard from him again.

The world felt surreal. What was he doing, sitting at his desk conducting business when life was crashing down around him? When his cell phone rang inside his pocket, he nearly jumped out of his seat.

"Charlie?"

"Sorry, Drake, just me." Ron's voice was heavy with concern. "I just got back to the office. Had a thought. A way we might get some info out of APD."

"Anything."

"Kent Taylor. He's one of my few contacts there. He might get us something."

"Homicide?"

"I know, it's not his case and I don't know how much he could find out. But it's worth a try."

"Make the call."

Drake fidgeted as the minutes ticked by. If he could just be airborne . . . if only— But that kind of thinking was useless. He could burn thousands of gallons of fuel and not make a bit of difference. More than two hours were gone now and the robbers could be just about anywhere in the state of New Mexico. This wasn't going to be one of those chases caught on video from a police helicopter—or his own, for that matter. He threw down the pen he'd been tapping relentlessly against a notepad, got up and paced the length of his office.

His stomach growled, reminding him that he'd never eaten breakfast but he couldn't imagine wanting food. Charlie was out there, probably scared and hungry. He paced to the kitchen and stared at the cupboards but nothing appealed. The empty spot near the fridge, where the dog's bowl used to sit, tugged at him. Since they'd lost their old red-brown retriever two months ago the routine of their days just wasn't the same. Charlie had gone into a deep funk for awhile, but pulled herself away from it by reasoning that the dog's time had simply come. Everyone gets old and leaves us eventually, she'd said.

Drake caught the tightness in his throat at the thought. What if Charlie didn't live long enough to grow old? What if—? He yanked his mind off that track. He could *not* start thinking that way.

He caught a glimpse of their neighbor, Elsa Higgins, through the kitchen window. An avid gardener, even though she was close to ninety, she spent a few hours nearly every day with her flowers and vegetables. She didn't know yet that Charlie was missing, and he couldn't bring himself to tell her. Luckily, the media hadn't gotten hold of the story yet. Another reason he wanted to speak with the police and federal agents—it was crucial that they not give out Charlie's name. Hearing it on the news would send their elderly neighbor over the edge. Surely Charlie would be home again before it became necessary to tell everyone about this.

His cell phone vibrated once more and he grabbed for it.

"Me again," Ron said. "Kent Taylor agreed to check with the guys in Robbery and see where things stand."

"So, what does that mean? More waiting?"

"Taylor is in his office right now. I'm willing to go down there, barge in and see what we can learn."

"I'm with you. Give me ten minutes."

He hung up the phone, his thoughts flitting everywhere. Charlie would call his cell before trying their home phone anyway. And, he remembered belatedly, he could forward any calls. He quickly punched the series of numbers to set the land line to send everything to his cell, then raced out the door.

It was all he could do to stay close to the speed limit and when he pulled up in front of the gray and white Victorian that housed RJP Investigations, he screeched to a stop and honked the horn. Ron's face appeared at an upstairs window and he signaled that he'd be right down.

It took ten minutes to get to the main police station downtown, another fifteen to park and make their way through the security that surrounded the inner workings of the department. Kent Taylor greeted them. Drake noticed that he seemed genuinely concerned for Charlie, even though he knew she'd been a pain in the man's neck on several occasions.

"All I've been told is that the suspects were masked and unidentifiable. The truck was a red Ford pickup truck without plates. Since it's not my department I'm only getting the basics."

"I want to talk with Dave Gonzales and Cliff Kingston," Drake said. "Where are they?"

"Upstairs—Robbery Division. They've set up a communications room where all the data is being processed and both agencies can work together."

"Take us there." It wasn't a request.

Taylor's gaze traveled from Drake to Ron and back. "I doubt they'll tell you anything."

"Just take us there." Drake's voice had a determined edge.

"Don't do anything stupid, Drake." Taylor shifted posture, displaying the holster strapped over his white dress shirt.

"Don't be ridiculous. I'm not armed. I just need information."

Ron stepped between them. "Kent, he'll be fine."

The hastily set up communications center buzzed with voices and Drake could see a cluster of men around a phone bank, with another group standing before a huge bulletin board on the wall. Taylor walked them in and introduced them.

The FBI man, Kingston, stepped over and shook hands. "Drake, sorry we don't have better news yet." He indicated a bank of video monitors on a table. The screens were solid blue. "We've been reviewing the security tapes from the bank."

"Can we see them?" Ron asked.

Kingston backed up the tape and hit a button. "This camera is behind the tellers, facing the customer area of the lobby."

Drake could see Charlie speaking to Gina, smiling at something the young teller had said. Something caused her to turn her head, her features twisted with concern. Gina's right hand slid under her cash drawer.

"She's the teller who hit the silent alarm," Kingston said. "Here's where the men come into view. Two of them."

Both wore ski masks. The chubbier one rushed in and took a stance at the north end of the row of teller stations. His body conveyed tension as he held a pistol stiff-armed in front of himself. The gun was aimed at Charlie. The other man—lean and of medium height—seemed to be shouting orders, although the video had no sound. He waved a gun toward the tellers and tossed canvas bags over the counter, toward them. His movements were quick—get in, get out, scare the hell out of everyone in the room.

A woman came out of a side office, from behind a closed door, her face registering shock when she realized what was happening. "Manager," Kingston said. She lowered herself to the floor the moment the hyper gunman turned on her. He kept shouting, making hand motions to hurry up the tellers.

Just when it seemed that the two men might dash out the door and the whole scary event would end, the hyper one said something to the stockier one and he grabbed Charlie by the arm.

The whole scene became unreal for Drake. With a gun jammed against her cheek, Charlie had no choice but to stumble along with the men. They moved out of range of the camera.

Kingston paused that tape and activated another. It showed the bank's door, with the customary markings on the doorjamb. He paused the tape long enough to point out that the leader was about the same height as Charlie at five foot, seven inches, while the chubbier man, the more passive one, was closer to six feet. He started the tape again. In the brilliant glare of sunshine, a crew cab truck waited with both passenger side doors open.

"That tape becomes unclear once the suspects are beyond the outer door." Kingston started a tape on a third machine. "This cam is outside."

The view showed a section of parking lot, the sidewalk in front of the bank, and the driveway to the street.

"We went back and looked at the vehicles arriving. The red truck drove in like anyone else, parked in a slot near the door. There's some vague movement inside the vehicle, the men talking, maybe slipping on their masks. There's glare on the windshield so we never do see their faces. Two guys get out and leave their doors standing open. While the two men are inside, the driver backs around and positions the truck so that the open doors are ready for the getaway."

He hit the Play button and the video picked up as the men rushed to the truck. The leader flung the money bags into the back seat and then jumped into the front and slammed the door. The second guy forced Charlie into the back, crawled in after her and the truck sped out with the back door closing as they hit the ramp of the driveway.

Drake's chest tightened as he watched his Charlie being taken away.

"Notice that there were no plates on the truck," Kingston was saying. "No bumper stickers or other identifying marks."

"What about running a DMV check, narrowing the results to red Ford trucks?" Ron asked.

"We're doing that but there will be hundreds."

"It's a 1982," Drake said.

"You sure about that?"

"I had one. Same model, exactly. Mine was black."

Kingston gave him a thoughtful look. "That's going to help a lot." He raised an index finger. "Just a second."

The paunchy FBI man rushed over to another agent who was sitting at a bank of phones on a large worktable. They exchanged a few words and then Kingston came back.

"We're getting right on it."

Drake felt marginally better, mainly because the lawman seemed more confident.

"You guys want some coffee?" Kingston gestured toward an urn on a side table.

Drake shook his head. He felt too wired already. Ron made his way toward the table and began shaking sugar from a glass container with a little hole in the top into his Styrofoam cup.

Kingston's cell phone rang and he excused himself to take the call. Drake gazed around the room. Everyone was busy doing something—none of that laid-back ambiance you saw in cop shows, where they seemed to have time to laugh and joke. In addition to the uniformed officer who was presumably on the phone with the Motor Vehicle Department right now, a couple others were speaking intently at other phones, taking notes. He meandered out into the hall and back, mainly to keep moving. He felt that time was slipping away.

One of the FBI men stood before the big bulletin board, drawing lines and scratching notes with the scant information they had. Drake's breath caught when the guy stuck Charlie's photo up there—the photo Drake had given them this morning at the bank. Never one for having studio portraits done, she'd culled this one from their honeymoon pictures near Taos and had given it to him for his wallet. She was wearing a heavy green parka and her cheeks were pink with the cold. She'd removed her sunglasses while he snapped the photo and the sudden brightness made her squint more than usual. He swallowed and turned to see that Cliff Kingston was headed his direction.

"This could be a real break," the FBI man said. "Knowing the year of the truck's first registration has brought us up a list of only about a dozen. Tracking the VINs we'll see how many are red—assuming someone along the line didn't repaint it a different color."

What was it with this guy? Gives you a tiny scrap of good news, only to qualify it with some reason it might not be valuable. Drake shook off the thought—any news was good news at this point.

"Then we can track registrations, see if any of those owners are in—"

One of the uniformed men grabbed Kingston's attention with an exclamation. He clicked a few keys at the computer where he sat and then stretched sideways to pull pages off a printer. He waved the sheets toward Kingston, who practically sprinted over to get them. Maybe the old federal agent wasn't so tired and burned out after all.

Drake stepped over to his side, trying to get a glimpse of the printed pages the man was scanning so intently. Dave Gonzales, the detective who'd spoken to Drake at the bank, walked in and joined them.

"Any names jump out at you?" Kingston asked, handing over the sheets.

Gonzales read through them carefully. "A couple." He started at the top and looked again, making Drake feel like shaking him.

"Let's sit," Gonzales said.

They flowed over to the long worktable, Drake and Kingston taking seats on either side of Gonzales, Ron coming along and sitting opposite. The detective pulled out a pen and made marks beside a couple of names.

"I remember some possession charges associated with this one, Joey Baca. They call him Jo-Jo. Mainly into moving small amounts of marijuana and coke. Never seems to have enough that we can really put him away for a long time."

"We're after bank robbers here," Kingston reminded.

Thank you, Drake thought, impatient at wasting time with the unimportant.

"We'll have to go to the computer to be sure," Gonzales said. "It's a big enough city that I don't hear about everything."

He realized that his tone had become snippy. "Sorry. Look, let's just wait for the searches to finish."

Luckily, the man who'd come up with the registration list seemed to be having some positive results. He brought Kingston another list. "Vehicle registrations that match your criteria, narrowed to owners with at least one arrest."

"There are only three. Don't know yet if the trucks are red, but we've got addresses."

Chapter 8

I'm swimming up from some gray, hazy place. Semi-conscious, drifting, moving. Belted into the back seat of a car . . . winding road . . . voices.

". . . she's making noises in her sleep." The guy with the shaky voice, the one guarding me.

I drift away again.

". . . awake yet?" Some more words, can't understand them. The hard guy with the black hair. String. Why would a person be called String? My mind can't work it out, just wants to sleep.

I want to snuggle into the far corner of the car and rest, but bumps in the road keep jostling me awake. Can't get comfortable. Those voices.

"Alamosa, pretty soon." The driver, I think. Not sure.

My head starts to feel a little clearer. Alamosa? Colorado. They're taking me across the state line. I can't quite decide if that's a good thing or a bad thing. Stiffer penalties for them, I imagine. Harder for the Albuquerque authorities to find me. I allow myself to slip away once more.

When I came back to consciousness, fully, it was nearly dark outside. It felt like the car was slowing. A pleasant dream vanished—I'd been with Drake looking at puppies, cute little guys. I eased my eyes open, peering through nearly-closed lashes, aware of male voices, finally remembering the bank and how I'd been taped up inside a red truck. But we weren't in the truck any more. Fragmented memories came back. Switching to a sedan, two gunshots, the leader of the group—String—coming out of a house somewhere, handing out sandwiches and telling the driver which direction to take.

The sandwich. I'd been drugged.

My nerve endings suddenly went on alert. What had happened while I was out? How many hours were gone now?

"At least a million for each of us," String said. "She's famous. Melinda said she was in the middle of shooting a movie somewhere in New Mexico. Musta been why she happened to be in that bank."

Oh, god. I'd forgotten that part, the part where these guys thought I was some famous movie star. Thought they could get a huge ransom for me.

"Well, well, looks like the little lady is waking up." String turned in his seat and stared at me.

Part of me wanted to go back to faking sleep, just to hear what they would say. Part of me wanted to really go back to sleep, wanted to wake up in my own bed and find out this whole day had been a nightmare.

"Have a good nap?" he asked.

A chill crept up my spine. If we hadn't been in a moving car . . . if he weren't more concerned with how much money this Cristina person was worth . . . I had a sick feeling about this guy String. And under the influence of whatever he'd put into my sandwich . . . he could have done anything at all.

I glared at him, not answering.

"Umm, she's a spunky one," Mole said. "Might have to get me some of that."

"Forget it!" String's order echoed through the car. He turned toward me again. "No, we're gonna take real good care of this lady. She's gonna be my ticket to an early retirement."

Sounded benevolent enough, but any trust on my part was quashed by the expression on his face—pure evil.

He turned back to Mole and gave terse directions that took us off the paved road and onto a long, straight stretch, some kind of farm road.

I did a quick assessment. Hands still bound with duct tape, legs free. No blindfold or gag—but that could change as soon as we got near other people. They wouldn't take the chance of my screaming for help. As long as they thought I was worth a decent amount of ransom I was probably safe, so even though I had to tamp down my inclination to protest the mistaken identity I'd be smarter to play along with them. And I couldn't take a chance on being drugged again. Had to come up with some kind of plan to get around that. They obviously didn't want me knowing where we were, but that was the most important information I could possess if I could somehow get a call out to the authorities or to Drake.

"That's the place," String said. "Pull around back."

The headlights flashed across the façade of a house, wavering away as we hit a dip in the dirt lane. From my backseat position I caught the merest impression of a two-story wood structure, a yard overgrown with weeds, a few large trees. Not a single light came from its interior. As Mole steered the car around the right side of the building I got a glimpse of a broken-out window.

I tried to think like a kidnapped movie star might—without a clue how that might go—make them think they really had the person they wanted.

"What the hell *is* this place?" I whined. "I expected at least a decent hotel." Would I be pushing it to request a poolside room and a plush robe? It *was* getting pretty chilly out for the light cotton shirt I'd put on this morning.

Beside me, Billy looked stumped, unsure whether he should answer.

String turned in his seat and shot me a hard stare. I dropped the spoiled-starlet routine and shut my mouth.

Mole whipped the car around to an open area at the back of the house and hit the brakes with a little more force than necessary. I didn't brace myself quickly enough and slammed against the shoulder harness. The breath left my lungs with a grunt.

"Listen, little bitch," said String. "First, you were our ticket out of the bank but now I'm only treatin' you nice for the money. I don't even have to deliver you in one piece. So you stay quiet. I got plenty of tape left if I get sick of hearing your voice."

Okay. Guess that put me in my place.

"Got it?" His eyes had narrowed to slits again.

I nodded slowly but my thoughts went something like this: You are *so* going to regret this, Mr. String. I'll get away and you'll be in prison. Or worse. Then I went off on a mental tangent in which I had the pleasure of shooting him in that part of his anatomy which would hurt the worst.

He'd turned around before a tiny grin touched my lips.

Billy caught it though and I worked at turning my expression into something resembling fright. Better not to let any of them get the idea that I had plans.

"Okay, get her inside," String ordered. He'd already opened his door and was standing up to stretch.

While Billy escorted me up a set of rickety wooden steps, String ordered Mole to toss him the car keys. He grabbed the bank bags from the trunk. Mole tried the back door, found it locked.

"No big deal," said String, picking up a baseball-sized rock from the yard and using it to bash out a pane of glass near the doorknob. "Instant house key. Grandma wouldn't have minded."

Which answered my question about how he knew where this place was and how he knew it would be empty.

String led the way inside, with Billy ushering me in next, Mole taking up the rear. So far, they weren't taking any chances on my tagging along behind and making a run for it. String flipped a light switch several times before he believed it wasn't going to work. From the looks of the place, I'd guess that it had been empty and the power cut off years ago.

We were in a celery-green kitchen, which still contained a white stove and round-shouldered refrigerator along with a chrome and linoleum table and four chairs padded in red vinyl, vintage 1950s. He dumped the money bags on the table and then walked over to the stove and found matches, striking one and holding it to a burner. It actually lit. Apparently the propane tank wasn't entirely empty. He used the bluish light to see while he rummaged through drawers until he came up with some candles. He lit two of them from the gas flame.

"It's better this way," he said to Mole. "Just my luck somebody'd come around if they spotted lights. We'll stay at the back of the house. No using the living room."

Mole and Billy nodded. String walked through a doorway just off the kitchen. A few seconds later I heard the distinct sound of steady stream hitting a dry toilet bowl. He moaned a sigh of happiness and returned, zipping up.

"It don't flush but who cares. Not gonna be here all that long."

Each of the other men took their turns before it occurred to anyone to ask if I needed to go. As repugnant as the idea was, using the facility right after them, I didn't have much choice.

"May I have my hands untied?" I asked. "It's a little hard to . . . uh . . ."

String flashed a look toward Billy, who drew out a knife and sliced the duct tape. Being able to lower my arms to my sides felt so good that I momentarily forgot my other need.

"No closing the door," String said.

"Where would I escape to? Even if I got outside I don't have a clue where we are."

He pulled his pistol from his waistband and aimed it loosely in my direction. "Fine. Close the door. But I'll be right here. One unusual noise and I'll blow that door down."

Oh, great. That was a nice image, knowing that he'd be right there listening to every sound I made. I sent him a defiant stare and closed the bathroom door firmly behind me. The small room was pitch black and I had to feel my way around. It was one of those experiences that I figured I'd either laugh about later, or I would block out as a result of post traumatic something-or-other. Even though they leered at me when I came out, I held my head high, flounced across the kitchen and sat in one of the chairs with my arms crossed over my chest as I imagined the real Cristina might do. Take that.

"We got any food here?" Mole asked, opening cabinets and poking around.

String looked a little put out but he obviously hadn't planned a menu for the evening, so he didn't answer.

Mole found a packet of saltines, still sealed, and a small jar of peanut butter. I wasn't having anything to do with peanut butter after that sandwich at lunch so I didn't even watch as he pulled out a table knife and began making himself a snack.

"When we gonna count the money?" Mole mumbled through a mouthful of goo.

"Right now," String said.

"What about Ollie?" Billy asked, for which he received a deadly glare from the boss. Billy shrugged. "Guess he doesn't have to be here. We can still count out his share."

"Yeah. We'll do that." String grabbed up one of the sacks and, losing patience with the cord that ran through the top of it, slashed the side of the bag with his knife.

I vacated my seat at the table, as the men shoved their way into position around it. Packets of banded cash plopped onto the table. String pushed it aside and sliced into the second bag. Red dye flowed over the money and coated String's hands before he could drop it.

"Dammit! Dammit to hell!" he shouted.

I backed up against the far wall as he raced to the kitchen sink. But without electricity to run the pump and the pump to deliver water to the house . . . well, he was screwed. He grabbed at a rumpled old towel, wiping frantically at his hands and cursing up a storm.

It was my chance. Mole and Billy were riveted to the scene, watching String deal with the blood-like substance. I edged toward the back door. Got one hand on the knob, turned it slowly. The old metal let out a squeal.

Chapter 9

Ollie backed away from Sissy's house, reeling from the sight of his aunt and her daughter lying on the living room floor, each with a neat round bullet hole to the head. He bumped into the parked white Pontiac, slumped against it. What the hell?

Suddenly, the surrounding high desert was way too noisy, with the screech of cicadas and the hum of the windmill out behind the house. He strained to listen for vehicles. What if the sheriff showed up? What if a neighbor saw him at the house?

He had a strong urge to get right back in the car and get the hell out of here.

Something held him back.

It couldn't be coincidence that Melinda and Sissy lay dead in the house on the same day that String and the gang robbed the bank. Ollie was no brain but he could figure out that when String said 'change of plans' he probably meant hooking up with Melinda. She had a decent car and the plan all along had been to abandon the red truck soon after the robbery. So where was the truck?

He pushed himself away from the Pontiac and headed toward the barn. The tall door creaked open. In the gloom sat String's red pickup truck beside Sissy's Jeep. It all began to make sense. He tried to remember what Melinda's car looked like—some little foreign four-door thing. Silver or gray or something like that. If it wasn't a muscle car or a truck, Ollie usually didn't notice details.

He chewed at the tips of his mustache, thinking. Where would they go?

He discarded the idea of their going back to Albuquerque. Once they'd gotten this far away they wouldn't take the chance.

How well did he know the other gang members? Mole, pretty well. They'd been neighbors in Albuquerque for a few years, hooked up when he discovered Mole was a pretty good source for pot. Whenever Ollie had a little money he could count on Mole to supply him. They'd had some pretty intense conversations, stretched out on plastic lounge chairs in Mole's backyard, taking a few hits, staring at the stars and contemplating the universe. As far as Ollie knew, all of Mole's relatives lived in Albuquerque; he couldn't think of anyone Mole would turn to this far north.

String—Ollie had only met him this spring, through Melinda. She was one of those girls who'd been in and out of Ollie's life since they were kids. Sometimes she lived with Sissy—that's when they would usually cross paths—other times she went off with her dad. Ollie didn't even know who that was.

But this spring she'd been back in New Mexico and this older guy, String, was with her. He was one of those scary men who wore all black and talked like he'd killed people. Short and wiry, which might have been the reason for his nickname, but he let Ollie believe it came about because he'd been known to string up his enemies, choking them until they did what he wanted—or until they died. Ollie left the myth intact. What did he know anyway?

Domino—he knew nothing about that guy. He was twenty-three; Ollie'd heard him tell Mole that. Worked at a pizza place. Had that soft look—like he ate way too many pizzas. Or like his mama still coddled him a lot. He'd just turned up one day and started doing things with the group. Somehow got invited along to do the bank job.

Ollie stared at the red truck, no closer to an answer. String was the leader, though, and wherever they went it would be his choice. So it would be somewhere String felt safe. A relative or a pretty close friend. He closed the barn door and slowly turned back toward the house, debating what to do next.

He couldn't go anywhere without some money. Sissy wouldn't mind.

The stench from the house was becoming noticeable in the afternoon heat. Must be over ninety outside. And the flies were swarming in a thick black cloud around the door. He batted them aside and pulled the neck of his T-shirt up over his nose and mouth before he stepped inside.

The sight of Sissy, lying on her back with her eyes wide open, tugged at him. She'd always been good to him as a kid. Brought him little Hot Wheels cars and stuff. Took him out for a burger now and then, just the two of them. He squeezed his eyes shut. She shouldn't end up like this.

He knelt beside her and ran a hand over her eyelids, easing them closed. Glanced over at Melinda. She lay on her side, half turned, like she'd belatedly decided to run. But she'd never had a chance. The bullet to her head had stopped her in her tracks.

Ollie stood up. Gotta get out of here, he thought. There's always the chance that somebody called the cops about this. He turned and surveyed the room.

A purse sat on the sofa and he grabbed it up and rummaged inside. Came up with a cell phone and a wallet. Pulled all the cash and Melinda's debit card from the wallet, pocketing them in a quick move. Stuck the cell phone in the other front pocket of his jeans.

Glancing around the room he spotted Sissy's purse on the kitchen counter. Retrieved more money. Debated about searching the house for more cash—surely she kept a little handy—but decided it was too risky to hang around.

Outside, he took a deep breath and cleared his lungs. Man, that was awful in there. He stared at the Pontiac for a full minute. Should he switch vehicles here, hot wire the truck or take Sissy's keys? Decided not. The truck was too identifiable with the robbery, and once Sissy's body was discovered the last place you'd want to be was driving her Jeep. The old white junker was the most anonymous.

Colorado. For some reason the word jumped into his head. But he felt a headache coming on when he pushed to think about it.

Ollie sat in the car for a minute, taking stock. He counted the cash. A little over two hundred—plenty for gas and some more food. He put it all in his wallet. Left Melinda's cell phone on the passenger seat.

Taking the debit card was a stupid move. Almost

anywhere he used it, he'd be on some security camera. He held it out the window, tempted to fling it aside. But you never knew. Might be good for a one-time use, if he really got desperate before he found the guys and got his share of the bank money. He put the card in the glove box.

Heat radiated off the hood of the Pontiac and Ollie suddenly felt a panicky need to get out of there quick. He forced himself to calm down and take it easy as he started the car, holding his breath until he heard the reassuring clack of her pistons. He eased away from the house and down the sandy lane, careful not to kick up a dust cloud.

At the paved road he paused and debated. Santa Fe or Las Vegas? He knew this part of the state pretty well from one summer of driving a soda delivery truck. Colorado. Again, he thought of it. What was the connection?

Okay, he thought. Turning right, heading toward Vegas, he'd end up passing through Raton, into Trinidad, eventually Denver. Taking a left, through Santa Fe, up to Española . . . you could end up due north in Alamosa or farther west, maybe Durango. The rural roads, smaller towns—that felt more like what String would choose. He took the left.

Driving along, he ran the names of towns through his head. There was some connection, if only he could think of it. Somebody String knew in Colorado. No, somebody he used to know there. A relative . . . an aunt? No, a grandmother. He'd once mentioned a family farm. This was back in the early planning stages of the bank job. Ollie struggled to remember the conversation.

All four guys sitting around Mole's dining table, they'd decided which branch of the bank, a smaller one in a pretty quiet part of the city. Talking about what to do next, where to go. String almost reminiscing about his grandma's farm, saying it was out in the country, away from town, isolated from neighbors. Then he'd quickly changed the subject. String wasn't the kind of guy who revealed himself, talked about his past or his family. In the blink of an eye the plan changed to one where they would head for Texas, get lost in the maze of farm roads and little bitty towns out there.

And now the plan had changed again.

Back to what String originally talked about?

Ollie got a strong feeling about it. String would choose a place he knew well, a place where he could take charge. Get rid of his partners—hell, he'd already cut Ollie out as far as he knew—take all the money for himself. And this place was . . . Ollie closed his eyes for a few seconds, studying the map in his mind, thinking of the roads. His tires hit the rumble strip at the edge of the road and he over-steered, drawing the wrath of a black BMW that roared by with its horn blaring.

Alamosa. It came to him in that way a memory will do in a moment when you're not concentrating too hard.

The sun dipped low in the sky, blasting the left side of his face as he headed into Española. He'd stayed to the back roads, forced himself to mind the speed limit. No law enforcement types knew about this car, but it wouldn't be smart to draw their attention. He couldn't be sure that someone hadn't seen him entering or leaving Sissy's property, and eventually someone would discover the bodies.

Lights beckoned from the row of fast food places along the town's main drag. Ollie's stomach rumbled, reminding him that his cheeseburger and fries were long gone. With money in his pocket and a healthy eighteen-year-old's appetite, he pulled into the drive-through at the Taco Bell and ordered the family dinner special.

Parked among hundreds of vehicles in the nearby Wal-Mart parking lot, he wolfed down seven tacos and two burritos before it occurred to him that there were no more food places for a long way. Maybe he should conserve. He put the other two burritos and the single remaining taco back into the sack and folded the top closed.

The map of the area ran through his head and he chose the route of least traffic that would get him to Alamosa, Colorado. As he wound through the mountains and the quiet villages along the way he let himself dream again about the bank money and a future with Rena Lynn.

It was completely dark now, blacker than a witch's underwear, aside from the occasional isolated house. The big meal and his lusty thoughts about Rena Lynn put Ollie into a mellow mood and he caught himself nearly dozing. He blinked awake. The short catnap he'd caught at the motel in Texas did nothing to offset the pre-dawn rising. Didn't even feel like the same day. He couldn't remember a time he'd been awake before dawn in his whole life. He nodded again.

Dammit—can't fall asleep at the wheel. He took a huge slug from the soda that came with his meal, swished it around so the fizz filled his mouth, swallowed it too fast and started coughing. By the time he got over feeling like he would choke to death at least he wasn't sleepy.

The Pontiac was getting low on gas again by the time he crossed into Colorado and he'd not noticed it at the first little town, Antonito. He crossed his fingers and edged toward Alamosa, the night getting darker and the gauge pointing lower.

At the first lit-up gas station he coasted in on fumes, breathing a sigh of relief. It was one of those outdated places where you had to go inside and pay first—no credit cards at the pumps—but since Ollie was paying in cash that was fine with him. An old guy sat on a stool behind the counter, looking like he was happy for the chance to take the load off.

"Gotta fill up," Ollie said. "Not sure how much she'll take." He peeled off forty dollars and the old guy gave him a skeptical look. He added another twenty.

The tank swallowed fifty-four dollars and eight cents and he'd be damned if he would leave the old coot that much as a tip. He went back inside for his change.

"Hey, I'm looking for an old friend." It had just occurred to him that prowling around in hopes of finding String's grandmother's place was probably pushing his luck too far.

The old man counted out Ollie's change the old fashioned way. "Yeah?"

"Guy named String—uh, Stringer. Said his family had a place here."

"Yeah, the Stringer Farm. Potato growers. Like ever'body here." The man closed the cash drawer. "But they ain't here no more. Elvira Stringer was the last one and she died three years ago. Place is all run down. Nobody livin' there."

Ollie wanted to ask a bunch more questions but thought better of it. The gas guy might be old but he looked pretty sharp.

"Oh, sorry to hear that. Well, thanks anyway."

He walked back to the Pontiac, feeling the old man's eyes on his back the whole way. He coaxed the car to life and pulled out slowly. Now what? Couldn't very well find the place if he couldn't ask around. And somebody who died three years ago wouldn't be in the phone book. He cruised into town, debated getting a room at one of those motels along the highway. They looked pretty new, fancy compared to the Shady Rest.

What am I thinking, he chided himself. String's around here someplace. I gotta find him before he decides to take off again. He scanned each of the motel parking lots, watching for a sign of Melinda's faded silver sedan but didn't spot it. He'd hit the far western edge of town and was debating turning around to scout out what the north end and the east end might hold, when he spotted the sign.

STRINGER FARM
The Best Colorado Potatoes
1.2 mi.

The blue lettering was faded and chipped against its white background, and the sign hung a little crookedly. Looked like one of its four bolts had come out and another was pretty loose. A red arrow aimed down a road to Ollie's left.

Ollie drove as far as the first bend in the road so the car would be out of sight from the highway. Turned off the lights and ignition and listened to the overwhelming quiet. He had no idea whether the 1.2 miles meant the edge of the farm's acreage or if that would take him straight to the house, but he didn't dare drive the noisy Pontiac any closer. He fortified himself with a very long drink from the giant soda cup, stepped to the side of the road and relieved himself of what he'd drunk earlier, then set off on foot.

He followed the dirt lane, sticking to the edge just in case, but it was a long one and he heard nothing but crickets. He was almost upon the house before he saw it, a gray old ghost rising out of the fields in front of a cluster of tall trees. He halted and cocked his head to listen. Voices. They rose and fell faintly on the night air.

Scanning the black mass of trees and the slightly lighter bulk of the house, he spotted a flickering light from a side window. He stepped to the grassy verge of the road and took his time approaching.

String wouldn't be happy to see him but at that moment Ollie Trask didn't give a damn.

Chapter 10

Drake chafed, knowing the information was right there, just outside his reach. He wanted so badly to snatch the page from the FBI man, knew that wouldn't gain him anything. He drummed his fingers on the tabletop.

"People!" Kingston called out. "Over here! Time to put our heads together."

Dave Gonzales stepped up to hand out the orders. "Jones and Rodriguez, you take the first name on the list, Joey Baca. Bookman and Kess, you'll be looking up Calvin Painter. Sanchez and I will check out Lonnie Stringer. I'm passing out pages with their last known addresses, vehicle descriptions, rap sheets. They've all got records. All should be considered armed and dangerous."

He handed a page to each set of officers. "I'll be real surprised if the guilty guy is actually at home with the red truck sitting out front, but we've all heard the stupid criminal stories, so anything's possible. Just go in with your eyes open. If your suspect isn't home check with family, neighbors . . . well, you know the drill. We want to find that truck and the owner of it."

The teams headed out the door, leaving Drake feeling decidedly left out. He wanted so badly to ride along, to be there for the catch, but knew the odds of that happening soon were quickly diminishing. Bars of golden light shone long against the carpet, telling him it was getting late into the afternoon.

"It's a process, Drake," Ron said, joining him by the window. "It never works like in the movies. There's no skycam that can see every move the crooks make, no blinking red light on some map that shows where they are now."

Drake nodded. "I'm just not used to being so completely out of the action."

"I know," said Kingston. The FBI man walked toward them. "I read about your rescue of that kid up in the mountains last month. You did a great job for the Search and Rescue team."

"Thanks." His voice came out soft. He felt like he was drifting in a surreal world, that if he went to sleep he'd wake up beside Charlie in their bed.

"If it's any consolation, we haven't lost a hostage in a very long time," Kingston said. "These guys aren't sophisticated criminals. They've got petty records, for the most part. A bank robbery is a new thing to them. They don't know what they're doing. We will catch them."

Drake wanted to say that telling a victim's husband that she was in the hands of incompetent crooks rather than master criminals wasn't a whole lot of comfort. But nothing would be gained by alienating these guys—they were doing what they could.

"I'm gathering the rest of the team over at the table. Come join us," Kingston said.

Drake and Ron took seats along with the remaining APD officers and the FBI men.

"Okay, we've got officers out on the streets, checking for the vehicle. I have a good feeling about this, that our robbers are tied to one of those three red trucks." Kingston took a breath and straightened the edges of the pages before him on the table. "That said, I also think there's a pretty good chance that these guys will have changed vehicles by now. If they are anywhere in this city, it would be the only smart thing to do. If they got by one of our roadblocks they had to do it in another vehicle. Every law enforcement person in this state is watching for an older, red pickup truck."

"Did the roadblocks go up quick enough?" one of the uniforms asked.

Kingston's gaze lowered. "We can't be sure. Word got out quickly, yes. But this is an easy city to get around and that bank branch is less than four minutes to a freeway ramp. That, and fifteen minutes to reach the county line . . ."

"Air surveillance?" someone else asked.

"By the time helicopters were airborne, the truck could have easily been concealed. You know how that goes. Perps pull into a garage somewhere, stay put a couple hours, the helicopters haven't spotted anything and we can't keep them out there all day."

"But after a couple hours we've got better ground coverage, can catch them with a roadblock." The officer looked directly at Drake as she said it, obviously trying to relieve his worry.

"Bottom line," said Kingston, " they can't have left the state. Not in that truck anyway."

The meeting broke up as the officers took calls and attended to other tasks.

"Mr. Langston? Mr. Parker? How about a bite to eat? It's been a long day and that coffee won't hold you forever." Kingston subtly steered them toward the door. "My treat? Grab a sandwich somewhere?"

Drake didn't feel like he could handle food but his feet carried him along after the others. They walked a couple of blocks in the hot summer air. He had to admit that just getting out of the building revived him somewhat. And he surprised himself by putting away a sizeable steak sandwich.

"I know this has to be impossibly hard for you, Drake." Cliff Kingston wiped French fry grease off his mouth with a napkin. They'd graduated to using first names during the meal. "But I assure you that we do catch these types. They're criminals who've had a bit of luck with convenience store jobs, they do a few successful drug deals, they start to think they're pretty hot stuff. They have no clue that a bank robbery means they're dealing with an elite unit within the local police department and that they now have to face the FBI. They will screw up. We will catch them."

Drake sent him a level stare. "But will Charlie be all right when you do?"

The FBI man's cell phone rang and he snatched it out of his pocket. "Right," he said to the caller. He slapped some cash on the table. "Back to the squad room. We're getting results."

Dave Gonzales stood in the middle of the room,

running a hand over the faint stubble on his head while uniformed officers gathered around him. Drake, Ron and Kingston joined them.

"Okay, let's get to the new information," Gonzales said. He pulled three sets of mug shots from a folder on the table and stuck them up on the bulletin board. "Joey Baca. First suspect. Jones? Anything on this guy?"

The veteran officer shook his head. "Don't think so. We found him home, watching TV, his truck parked out front. Plus, Baca's taller and heavier than the guy on the security tapes."

Gonzales nodded. "Thought so. But we needed to check." He turned toward Officer Bookman. "Anything on Calvin Painter?"

Drake looked at the photo Gonzales was indicating. It showed an emaciated Anglo man, a guy with the hollow look of a cocaine addict.

"Nasty guy," Bookman reported. "But I don't think he's the one. Plus, his truck was up on blocks in the backyard. He claims it's been that way for more than a year and I tend to believe it."

"So, we're down to Lonnie Stringer, the guy Sanchez and I went to check on. I've got a strong feeling he might be our perp. Sanchez, you want to fill them in?"

The younger officer shuffled nervously, unaccustomed to being in the limelight with his peers. He pulled out a small notebook and read from it.

"Detective Gonzales and I drove to the suspect's last known address on Carlisle northeast. No vehicles were present outside the residence, and no lights were on inside. After knocking at the front door and announcing ourselves we circled the house but found no evidence of the truck in question." He glanced back at Gonzales. "Conversation with the neighbor to the north revealed that Stringer was renting the residence but has not been seen there in at least a week. The woman verified that Mr. Stringer does still own the red Ford truck and that he was driving it when he was last seen leaving his home."

Gonzales piped up. "So, Stringer's red truck seems the most likely among the ones we got the DMV hits on. The other reason I like him for this is his record. Fits what we've been thinking. Gang activity as a teen, graduated to convenience stores, arrests for armed robbery, did time in Santa Fe. His physical size matches what we saw on the security tapes.

"I pulled DMV records for Lonnie Stringer before I called everyone in," Gonzales continued. "His license photo is going out to all units in the city, and over the wires region-wide, already. Plus, I learned that he owns another vehicle, a white 1979 Pontiac. We're watching for that one, too. It's a good bet that he may have switched cars soon after the robbery. We've issued a BOLO for both vehicles. Plate numbers and full descriptions are in your packets."

He passed printed sheets around the table. "While our guys on the streets are looking for the vehicles, I want all of us to spread out and start asking questions. Find out this guy's haunts, his friends, his relatives. Who are the other two perps? And who are they turning to now, who's hiding them?"

Drake stared at the photo of the thin man with greasy black hair combed straight back off his low forehead. Beard growth shadowed his face, but did nothing to conceal the hard jaw and the cruel mouth. Stringer looked like the kind of guy who would clean up well and work the charm on some people, but underneath had a mean streak. Drake felt his gut wrench at the thought of this guy anywhere near Charlie.

The detectives were milling about in small groups, discussing plans, slipping on their jackets, getting ready to follow Gonzales's instructions. Ron stood near the door, probably wondering what he and Drake could do. The sitting around was killing them both.

Ron pulled out his phone and hit one of the speed-dial numbers, connecting right away with his girlfriend. Drake caught himself listening to their sweet-talk greeting. Victoria apparently asked about Charlie because Ron told her that the police didn't know much yet, and cautioned her not to talk to anyone about it. They ended the call with more loving words, leaving Drake with an empty core of envy inside.

He glanced up at the windows. It was fully dark out now. No chance to use his aircraft to accomplish anything. He wanted to race out the door, to track this guy and his cohorts and wring somebody's neck. Mostly, he wanted Charlie back, just to take her home and pamper her and hold her again.

Kingston approached and laid a hand on Drake's shoulder. "Might as well go home, guy. There's really nothing you can do here. Gonzales has already stuck his neck out, allowing you to be here at all. The Chief could cause him a lot of grief over that."

Drake nodded but the words soared past him. He stood up and looked around the room as if he were seeing it for the first time. Everything felt surreal.

Ron stood near the door, patiently waiting for Drake to head that direction.

"Let's go," he said.

They left the squad room together and walked to the elevator. Ron seemed a little restless but he didn't say a word in front of the two police detectives who were in the small enclosure with them. When the door opened at the parking garage level, the detectives went toward a plain city car.

"We gotta talk," Ron murmured, nudging Drake's arm. "Let's go to the office."

Drake unlocked his pickup and they got in. "So, tell me."

"I hung near the door up there, paying attention to little scraps of conversation."

"And?"

"Gonzales's partner, Sanchez, mentioned a name that came up in their conversation with Stringer's neighbor. Guy named Mole."

Drake steered out of the city parking garage, made some turns, and headed down Central Avenue. Ron and Charlie's office was only a few blocks away, in an old residential area near downtown.

"Mole is the street name of a guy named Leon Mohler. I've run up against him before. He's a bad dude—gang ties, drugs, prostitution, time in the pen. I want to check my files at the office and see what I've got, maybe an address or something." Ron stared out the side window, riding silently for a couple of blocks.

"Drake, he's as bad or worse than Stringer. I hope they're wrong about him being Stringer's partner. He's not the kind of guy I want around Charlie."

Chapter 11

"Stop her!" String shouted.

It took a second for the command to register with the other two, but by then String had reached for his pistol—dyed hands and all—and aimed it directly at my head.

"Get away from the door." His voice was measured and deadly.

I complied.

His arm came up, preparing to deliver a swift backhand to my head. I flinched, ready to duck, but he pulled back.

"Don't *ever* try that again." His voice went very quiet, ten times scarier than when he screamed at me. "You're gonna stay beautiful only as long as it takes us to get that big-shot producer of yours to fork over the cash. But you cross me . . . I don't give a damn if we deliver you to him in one piece or not."

He didn't have to remind me that he meant what he

said. I believed him.

Mole grabbed up the duct tape and wrapped it around my wrists so fast that it hardly registered.

"Do her legs too," String ordered. "And park her over there in the corner."

Mole shoved me to the gray linoleum floor beside the dusty green wooden cupboards, the very corner with no possible exit. He straddled my feet and wrapped the silver tape around my jean-clad legs. Then he did my ankles. He aimed a discreet kick at my hip as he stood up, but luckily he didn't connect with a lot of force. He laughed as he watched me squirm.

What would they do when they discovered I wasn't really Cristina Cross? I had the sick feeling that my life wouldn't be worth a hoot.

String reached for the cash on the table.

"Hey," said Mole, "that dye'll come off your hands and wreck the rest of it."

String halted in mid-reach and muttered something about trying to find some water to wash the stuff off his hands. He stomped out the back door with a parting shot to Mole and Billy that they better not touch the money while he was gone.

The other two eyed the pile of unspoiled money, their wheels clearly turning, wondering whether the third bag would come out a healthy green or be bloodied by that nasty red dye. I found a small degree of amusement in watching their expressions, just because otherwise there'd not been a whole lot of fun in this entire, horrible day.

String stuck his head in at the open door. "Find me some kind of pan or a bucket or something."

Billy began to look around the kitchen, coming up with a saucepan from one of the lower cabinets next to me. He carried it to the door where String waited impatiently.

"Thought I remembered my grandma having a rain barrel out here," he said. "Looks pretty full." He took the pan and came back a minute later, sloshing water on the floor.

"Domino, look in the bathroom and get me some more towels."

Billy hopped to, doing every little thing String ordered.

"Okay, I'll have this stuff off me in a second." He scrubbed at his hands but the red substance only seemed to spread. "Dammit. Where's some soap?"

Billy buzzed around some more, coming up with an old bar of something from the bathroom. It lathered up nice and pink on String's hands but the stain wasn't leaving. Eventually, he gave up with the washing action. He dried his hands and arms on a light-colored rag and not too much pink came off.

"I guess I can touch stuff now," he said. "Who wants to open the last bag?"

The others looked at him like he was crazy. I had a hard time not grinning.

"Just do it real careful," Mole suggested. "Maybe you can get the money out without that pack-thing busting."

"Me? Do I look like the only one here?"

"You the only one here with red all over you. Might as well keep the rest of us clean."

String send him a murderous look, but he reached for the third bag anyway. I rooted for the bag and sure enough, red goo exploded all over String's hands again. He let out a flotilla of words that would have made the sixth fleet proud.

I hid my face against my arms so they wouldn't catch me laughing.

He picked up the two spoiled bags and flung them into another room, still swearing like a madman. After another round with the soap and water and rags, everything from the biceps down was pretty well still crimson, but at least it wasn't rubbing off on everything he touched.

"I need a damn drink," he said, flopping into one of the chairs at the table.

Billy piped up. "I think your grandmother must have been a teetotaler. I pretty well went through the stuff in here and didn't find any booze at all."

String thought about it but didn't seem to come up with an answer.

"Let's count this. At least with some money, tomorrow we can get us some supplies."

There were murmurs of assent all around and the other two took seats at the table too. I watched from my corner of the floor, catching maybe half the action. Mole apparently didn't want to trust the bank's count on the wrapped packets of bills and he immediately pulled off the little paper bands. That created a good-sized pile of loose bills, in all denominations, and I seriously thought the men would come to blows a couple of times as they argued over the count. I didn't mention that I'm an accountant and pretty good with numbers. It was more fun to watch them muddle through it.

I lost interest a couple hours into the process so I spent my time figuring out how to get myself out of this mess. In retrospect, I might have been better off to make a run for it when I had my hand on the doorknob. It's hard to get an accurate shot with a pistol at a moving target so the odds of String actually hitting me were slim. Unfortunately, the other two men had been very close by and probably would have tackled me within ten feet of the back door. So, scratch that.

But if I ever got another chance, say, one guy guarding me—gun or no gun—I'd better think seriously about doing it.

The main thing that weighed on my mind right now—well, it was hard to narrow my zipping thoughts down to just *one* thing—was what would happen when they made their ransom demand of Cristina Cross's producer. Either Cross or the producer would react with puzzlement or an outright denial. Cross would step out in front of the cameras with her pretty face intact and say, "What kidnapping? I'm obviously alive and well and working on my new movie," at which point she'd launch into a live version of her new movie's trailer and I'd be toast.

Raised voices interrupted my thoughts. "This stash stinks. You call this a share? This job, it's turning into a gyp."

String's deadly voice stopped Mole's whining. "Enough, already! We got three stacks here. You take yours and be happy with it, or I'll give you a real reason to gripe."

Since he was waving the pistol around again, I had the feeling that the complainers would be silenced one way or another. There were some grumbles around the table but the overall tone was of acquiescence. I could see Billy stacking his bills, tamping them into neat little packets. Mole opted for the bulk cash approach, coming up with a pillowcase from another room and, after being sent to fetch more for the others, began jamming the money inside.

A noise grabbed my attention—the sound of stealthy footsteps on the back porch. Billy happened to be facing me and when he saw my riveted attention he froze. String and Mole snatched up their guns, spun and aimed.

The doorknob twisted and the door swung slowly open.

A young guy—I'd guess late teens—stood frozen in the doorway. His jeans and T-shirt were rumpled, his knees and brown leather boots crusted with dirt. It looked like he'd crawled hands-and-knees to get here. He had blond hair in a sort of grunge version of a Beatles cut and his narrow face sported a wispy Fu Manchu goatee.

He fixed pale blue eyes on the three men and the cash on the table. "Well, ain't this a cozy little scene."

Chapter 12

"Kid." String lowered his pistol slowly, and Mole followed suit. "Where'd you come from?"

"Thought I'd be in Texas, still sitting there in that motel, waitin' for y'all?"

Mole's gaze flicked over to String, silently asking permission to blow away the newcomer. Billy watched the leader's face, stayed alert, looked ready to duck.

"I found Melinda and Sissy," the young guy said.

String gave that a moment's thought. "Any cops around?"

"Nope." To his credit, the kid kept his composure. He stared at the money on the table. "Looks like you got it divided up three ways. Where's my share?"

This was the moment where I half expected String to simply raise his gun and do away with the problem. Oddly, he began to dissemble. "We was just starting to count it."

Mole gave him an incredulous look.

Billy shifted from one foot to the other.

It hit me. String couldn't be sure that the young guy hadn't called the police after he left Sissy's place, and now he was mentally scrambling to remember if he'd left any identifying clues behind. He thought of it about the same time I did—the truck.

"What'd you drive—coming here?"

"Pontiac."

"I never heard it."

The one he called Kid chuckled. "Yeah, old rattletrap don't exactly come up quiet, does she?"

That was the moment he happened to glance down and spot me, taped up and huddling on the floor.

"Who the hell is that?"

"That, Kid, is our fortune." String clapped a hand on the kid's shoulder. "We got us a hostage that happens to be worth a bundle."

Kid eyed me suspiciously.

"She's a movie star. Melinda told us. And in the morning we're hitting up her producer for enough money that we won't care that the stupid bank job didn't give us much."

Yeah, if the producer's account actually had any money in it. But checking up on one production company's finances was what had gotten me into this mess in the first place.

I could see the young guy trying to process all this. I couldn't figure out if he was sharper than he looked or if he truly was gullible enough to go along with the plan. He sent one more skeptical look my way before turning his attention back to the money. Evidently the proverbial bird in the hand and all.

"I want my share, String. Sissy woulda had your neck if

you cut me out."

I watched String carefully. Something in him folded. Weird relationship. He'd shot Sissy without a second thought, but now he would listen to this guy at the mere mention of her name . . . I puzzled over it as they shook the money out of the pillowcases and started the count all over again. Eventually I leaned against the cabinets and dozed.

Cold seeped up through the floor, and I woke up stiff and aching. The house was quiet. Pale daylight filtered down from the kitchen's only window. One man sat at the table now. Billy.

I must have groaned as I shifted position because he was staring at me. The pistol lay on the table within easy reach of his right hand. He made no move to touch it.

"Where's everybody?" I asked.

He nodded vaguely toward the other rooms. "Found 'em some places to sleep." He kept his voice barely above a whisper and I found myself following suit.

"Didn't you get to sleep?" I asked.

"A little. String said we should take turns watching you."

Watching me sleep, bound with duct tape? Now that was a creepy thought.

"I'm freezing down here. Any chance there's a blanket or a spare jacket around?"

He left the kitchen and came back a few minutes later with a thin bathrobe, which he draped over my shoulders. It looked like something from the '40s and smelled of old woman, but I reasoned that I wasn't exactly at my freshest right now either. At least it was something.

"So, String's grandmother lived here until she passed away, but no one ever came and cleared out her things?" I asked, by way of getting a conversation going.

Billy shrugged. "I don't know his family story."

"I need to stand up. My legs are all cramped."

Considering that I'd been folded to the shape of a backward capital N all night, it was amazing that I unfolded at all when Billy came over to give me a hand.

"Could I go to the bathroom before they all come back in here?" I pointed at the tape around my knees and ankles. "It would be quieter if I didn't have to hop the whole way."

"Just for a minute. And I'll have to tape you back up as soon as you're done." He fished a short knife from his pocket and slit the tape on my lower extremities. "Make it quick."

I limped across the room, every joint in my body screaming, and I closed the bathroom door behind me without asking permission. The tiny room reeked. I couldn't imagine how it would be after another few days of use by, now, five people. I held my breath and finished as quickly as I possibly could.

Taking my mind off the stench, I took a quick look around. The high, tiny window showed as a rectangle of pale gray, and there was a slim wedge of light from under the door. I could make out a porcelain tub, an old-fashioned sink mounted directly to the wall, a mirrored medicine cabinet above it. While struggling to get my jeans back up with my wrists bound together I edged toward it. Was able to pull the hinged mirror back, but the shelves inside revealed only a plastic comb and a few bottles. I couldn't read the labels in the dim light.

A tap at the door startled me.

"Hurry up, Miss Cross," Billy whispered.

I stepped back into the kitchen just as String entered from another doorway.

"What the—" he demanded, staring at Billy.

"Uh, sorry, String. She really had to go." He grabbed up the tape, made me sit in one of the chairs, and did a secure job of lashing my legs together again.

The boss looked like he had more to say but Mole showed up just then, with the new guy right behind.

"I'm hungry," the young one complained.

Tell me about it, I thought. I'd had nothing but a drugged peanut butter sandwich in the last twenty-four hours, and I'm a girl who's usually pretty prompt with her meals. A vision of chicken enchiladas smothered in green chile sauce flashed before me. Was this what I would think of in my dying moments—did my life truly consist of food?

String, meanwhile, flung open all the cupboard doors but didn't find anything. They'd consumed all the dry saltines last night.

"No coffee, no booze. What a load of—" Mole's little observation was interrupted by his boss.

"Okay, I've got a plan," String said. "We'll be able to hang out here for a few days if we get some food. And we gotta figure out how to contact somebody who's gonna pay to get our girl back." His eyes rested on me for a long moment, sending a trail of bile up my throat.

The young guy, Kid, spoke up. "I thought about that. I know who we can call."

We all stared at him.

"Rena Lynn follows that movie stuff all the time. *People* magazine, them entertainment shows on TV, all that. So, anyways, she's telling me awhile back that Cristina Cross is filming on location around Santa Fe. Rena Lynn wants to go up there and try out for some kinda bit part. I guess they hire locals to be in the crowds or something?"

"Yeah, so?" Mole gave him a hard stare.

"So, I could text Rena Lynn and ask her the name of the movie company. Get the phone number they put in that audition call thing."

String mulled this over. "That's not bad." He gave me a hard stare. "Or, we just beat it out of this one." He headed toward me with a balled up fist.

My nerve endings froze.

"String, wait!" Billy reached for his arm. "You said we better not mess her up. They might ask for a picture, you know, to prove she's alive. She better not have bruises all over her face."

"Good point." He lowered his aim and sent the punch to my gut instead.

Pain shot through my entire mid-section and my vision became a dark tunnel.

"String!" Mole spoke up. "Don't be dumb."

Well, that accusation took all the attention off me as String tackled Mole and the two men went to the floor. Luckily, Kid and Billy stepped in and pulled them apart before guns and knives appeared. I blinked to get my vision back and gasped for air, both from the blow and from the sudden way in which the whole precarious scene had changed.

After a minute or so the fighters went to opposite corners of the ring, glaring at each other, with the other two on watch that they didn't start up again.

"C'mon String, the plan's gonna fall apart if you guys fight." Billy sounded like the hopeful child who didn't want his parents battling anymore.

String took a deep breath, glared one final time at Mole, and spoke. "Yeah. Okay, let's get on with the plan then."

He sat at the table once more, ruby arms on its surface, scarlet fingers pressed together.

"Somebody's gotta stay here and watch her. Mole, you'll do that."

I *so* wanted to protest that choice but luckily Mole did it first. "Nuh-uh. I will be there when you make the ransom call."

"Okay, okay. Domino, you can watch her. Kid, go out there where you left my car and bring it up here by the house. Somebody'll spot it from the highway."

The young guy started to say something but thought better of it. He went out the back door.

I didn't want to point out that Billy was their worst choice to be my guard. He'd already gotten into trouble for untaping me once this morning. But I was no fool; if they chose Billy, I could go with that.

"And just to be sure she don't give you no trouble, she's gonna take a little nap again," String said, pulling a prescription pill bottle from his pocket. He tossed it to Billy. "Make sure she takes one before we leave."

A sound outside drew everyone's attention and a full minute later a vehicle with an extremely bad muffler drove around the back of the house. Now I understood why the young guy had chosen to approach on foot last night.

"Mole, grab some of your cash. Let's go."

"Hey, why do I have to pay for the—" Mole shut up when String picked up his pistol from the table and pointed it just a little too long toward Mole. After Mole stuffed some bills into his pockets, String jammed the gun into the waistband of his pants, without another word.

Mole and String went out the back door and I could hear them talking to Kid. Then the three of them got into the deceased Melinda's silver-gray sedan and it turned around and headed down the gravel lane.

Billy turned to me. "Well, uh, I think you better take one of these." He yawned as he held up the pill bottle and it occurred to me that he'd probably not slept all night, for fear of String's reprisals if he didn't guard me closely enough. He worked the cap loose and tipped a single tablet out into his hand, then gave it to me.

"I'll need water. I never could swallow pills dry," I told him.

He dutifully went out to the rain barrel and came back with a pan full, from which he poured some into a questionable-looking glass that he found on the counter. While he had his back turned I slipped the pill into the pocket of my jeans and then mimed popping it into my mouth when he turned around. I swear, some guys make this way too easy.

The water went down cool and good, reminding me that I was really dehydrated. I drank the whole glass and asked for more.

"Billy?"

He set the glass on the counter and turned toward me again. "Yeah?"

"I don't think I can fall asleep on that floor again. Isn't there a couch or something softer in this place?"

So far String had kept the two of us strictly in the kitchen and Billy seemed surprised by the idea that there was more of a house here.

"Sit there," he said. "I'll go check."

Like I had much choice. Hopping out the back door

with duct tape around my legs, ankles and wrists, in broad daylight, didn't seem like a real smart move, even in my desperate wish to be out of here.

He didn't go far to check anyway. Standing in the doorway he scanned the rooms beyond.

"Okay. There's a couch in the living room. We'll go in there."

I hopped noisily into the other room, hoping Billy would be unnerved enough by the thumping that he would unstrap my legs, but it was not to be.

I yawned hugely and fought an absurd urge to laugh when Billy automatically followed suit. Maybe I could coax him to sleep this way.

"Could you bring that robe from the kitchen for a cover?" I asked as I sat on the sofa, which turned out to be on the lumpy side. A small throw pillow rested nearby but it had a distinct head-indentation on it. I imagined Mole or String stretched out here during the night and everything in me rebelled at laying my head on the same spot. I flipped the pillow over and tried to think of anything else at all as I lay on my side, curled up.

Billy came back with the musty robe and draped it over me.

I did another pseudo-yawn. "Boy, those pills work fast."

I slowed my breathing and concentrated on keeping my eyes from moving under the lids. Billy moved away from me and I heard him flop into an overstuffed armchair that I'd noticed near the foot of the sofa. Perfect. With my eyelids barely cracked open I could spy through my lashes.

Sure enough, within ten minutes my guard was fast asleep. Unfortunately, when I tested the depth of his slumber by making a little groaning noise, he immediately snapped awake and eyed me suspiciously. When it became clear that I was probably just snoring, he nodded off again. Well, darn. There'd be no tippy-toeing past him and out the back door.

Like I was in any position to be subtle about my movements. So far my attempts at hopping from place to place were anything but quiet. I thought about my situation and found that applying logic was a way to suppress the panic that otherwise hovered at the edges all the time. I would need to: a) get them to trust me enough to leave my legs unbound—arms and legs would be even better; b) be very careful not to ingest any more of those sleeping pills—I would eventually need some real sleep but I wanted it on my own terms; c) watch for my chance as soon as possible—once the real Cristina Cross showed up alive and well my value was gone and my ass was grass.

That thought did nothing to ease my fears but forcing myself to relax and think, it seemed that now was a good time to rest up and bank away some energy. I finally drifted off to sleep.

Chapter 13

Drake woke with a start. The glow of a streetlight through the bay window reminded him that he was on the loveseat in Charlie's office. Yesterday's nightmare came back to him in a rush. He and Ron had come here after spending all afternoon at APD headquarters downtown. The FBI and APD Robbery Division were on the case. But Charlie was still missing. He patted his pockets. Her cell phone was in one, his own in another. Neither had rung all night.

He sat straight up, rubbing at his neck to ease a cramp from dozing off with his head at an odd tilt. It must be early morning. A clock on Charlie's credenza confirmed, 5:57. He scrubbed at his face, willing some blood to the surface. Where was Ron?

Drake wandered across the hall to his brother-in-law's office to find him seated at his desk, head on his arms, snoring away. He left him alone and went into the bathroom.

A glance in the mirror showed the ravages of the situation—dark circles under his eyes, stubble thick on his face. If possible, it seemed there was more gray in his hair; the touches at his temples had become generously sprinkled throughout the brown. He splashed water on his face and finger-combed the hair. Until he had Charlie back he really didn't much care how he looked. His eyes became red-rimmed thinking of her but he refused to give in. She'd be okay. He had to believe it.

He meandered downstairs to the kitchen, found the makings for coffee and started brewing a pot. Overhead, he heard heavy footfalls. He'd probably wakened Ron, but that was good. They needed to get moving.

Three minutes later Ron's boots sounded on the stairs. He came into the kitchen carrying a small sheaf of paper.

"Do I smell coffee?" he said.

Drake pointed to the burbling machine. "Almost ready. What's that?"

"Research." He handed Drake the pages but clearly he wasn't going to interpret them until he'd got some coffee in him.

While Ron rummaged through the cabinets for a couple of clean mugs, Drake paged through the sheets. They appeared to be printouts of internet pages.

The coffee maker hissed, a few drops hitting the hot metal plate, when Ron removed the carafe to pour. Drake took a first sip of the hot brew while Ron spent a minute doctoring his with sugar and creamer.

"How'd you find all this?" Drake asked, giving a nod toward the pages on the kitchen table.

"Started with what I knew. Same as any investigation."

He took a generous hit of the coffee. "Had the names of Lonnie Stringer and Leon Mohler. While the cops are out on the streets looking up known associates I opted for technology. Well, that and a little memory."

They sat at the table and Ron dealt the pages out like a hand of solitaire. He tapped at a photo.

"Leon Mohler. This one I knew because I'd run up against him before. So, I Google his name and come up with somebody who 'friended' him on Facebook. A woman named Lila Jackman. I know—who'd have thought criminals might have Facebook friends. But okay." He tapped at a picture of a dark-haired woman. "I take a look at this Lila's profile and she's got a *bunch* of friends. I start clicking on their profiles. Among them is a girl named Melinda Davies."

Drake knew his expression must look completely blank at this point. Charlie was the computer expert in their family, and even she had not gone much for this social media craze.

"Melinda is one of those chatty little types who thinks the entire world wants to know what she had for breakfast, when she went to the mall, that kind of stuff."

"People really open up that much?"

"You wouldn't believe." Ron got up for a minute to top off his mug. "So, chatty little Melinda, who posts about a zillion times a day, is talking about how her boyfriend is going to take them on a big trip. She's guessing maybe Europe, maybe a cruise, and her friends are all chiming in with their O-M-Gs and W-T-Fs and making guesses of their own about where this trip might go."

Drake shrugged, feeling more out of the loop than ever.

"Sorry. Anyhow, one of Melinda's friends is her mother,

Sissy Davies. Yesterday morning Melinda posts something. Here it is . . . 'tired of waiting around for String to show, heading to mom's place at R-ville.' The boyfriend's name is *String*."

"Stringer."

"Exactly. Makes sense to me anyway. These little bunches of friends tend to be inter-related and it would make sense that Melinda's boyfriend would also be a pal of Leon Mohler."

"Yeah, true."

"Maybe the most significant thing is that Melinda has not posted one word since yesterday, around noon. We're talking the queen of chatterboxes, and suddenly she's completely silent. I don't like it."

Drake stared at the photos, trying to process what Ron was telling him. "So, what next?"

"That's about the point, at three this morning, where my brain shut down and I guess I just dozed off at the desk."

Drake grinned at him. "Yeah you did. Me too, on Charlie's little couch."

"So, my first step this morning is to find Sissy Davies's address. That's where Melinda was headed when she dropped off the face of the earth. Why would she do that when she's expecting to hear from boyfriend Stringer at any moment with news of this big, special trip they're going to take?"

Drake felt his pulse quicken. It was the first concrete thing they had to go on. "Shouldn't we be reporting all this to Kingston or Gonzales?"

"Yeah, definitely. Let me see how much more I can gather before we contact them." Ron filled his mug a third time and headed upstairs, actually looking pretty much awake now.

Drake mulled over the new information while he rummaged through the kitchen cupboards to see if there might be anything they could call breakfast. A package of Oreos looked more appealing than the outdated milk and nearly empty orange juice carton in the fridge. He grabbed them and headed toward Ron's office.

"There's a Davies listed with a Romeroville address," Ron said. "First initial C."

"I've flown over Romeroville and it's not much. There can't be too many unrelated Davies there. If C doesn't translate to something that would be Sissy, this person will surely know who she is."

"My thoughts exactly." Ron picked up his phone and dialed.

"It's only six-thirty," Drake said.

"Yeah, so why isn't someone answering?" He sat with the phone to his ear and let it ring and ring. After two full minutes he hung up. "Not happening. No one's there."

"Or no one wants to answer. Maybe they have caller ID and you're coming through as an unknown or something. Or Melinda and her mom went somewhere, back to Melinda's place overnight . . . there are just too many possibilities."

"I'll check for a number for the daughter. As chatty as she is, Melinda probably gave her real location on Facebook, too." He moved his computer mouse and began clicking.

Drake's cell phone vibrated and he nearly jumped out of his shirt. He snatched it out of his pocket, hoping the unfamiliar readout number meant good news.

"Charlie?"

"Sorry, Drake, it's not." Cliff Kingston's voice sounded tired, as if the FBI man was another who'd not gotten much sleep last night.

"Is there any news?" Drake knew he sounded desperate. Hoped the cop picked up on it. If only they had pulled off a miracle during the night and had Charlie safely with them.

"Not much, I'm afraid. The detectives are still working on leads."

"We may have a few," Drake said, "but I still have a hard time grasping all the connections."

Ron wiggled his fingers, wanting Drake to let him talk to Kingston. He handed over the phone and listened as Ron put the story together concisely, telling about the links between Stringer, Mohler and the two Davies women. Kingston began to talk and Ron clicked to put the phone on speaker so Drake could hear.

"—agree that it's suspicious for Melinda to quit posting, given her history. I'll get someone out to the Davies place at Romeroville right away."

Ron asked a couple more questions of the FBI man but didn't learn anything new.

"Stay in touch," Kingston said as he ended the call. There seemed a grudging respect in his voice for Ron's investigative abilities, but at least the man was working with them rather than pulling rank and trying to cut them out.

"Ron, you said that Mohler had a Facebook page? Does it show an address for him, anything we could use?"

"Nah, checked it already. I'm guessing somebody set it up for him. There's no personal information beyond listing Albuquerque as his hometown."

Drake bit his lip, feeling stumped.

Ron had already helped himself to a couple of the Oreos but apparently they weren't hitting the spot. He suggested that they grab some breakfast at a diner he knew, over by the university. Without a better plan, Drake agreed.

The place was crowded despite the hour, full of students who looked bleary-eyed and a handful of business people, probably either traveling salesmen or local corporate types on their way to early office meetings. Drake didn't really care. He searched for Charlie's face everywhere he turned and was glad when they were shown to a booth near the windows so he had somewhere else to direct his attention.

"Good thing we had coffee at the office," Ron commented.

Drake had to agree. It took nearly a half-hour before someone came to take their order, even longer for the kitchen to produce the meals.

They'd no sooner received their food than Drake's phone rang. Once again his heart went into overdrive, but this time he recognized the number on the readout.

"State Police located the truck," Kingston said immediately. "In a barn on the Davies property." He paused, but there was more, Drake could tell. "Also found the bodies of Melinda and Sissy Davies."

"Oh, no."

Ron almost leaped over the table at Drake's tone, so he took a second to repeat Kingston's information.

"What about Charlie? Is there any—?"

"No sign. We're sending an FBI team up there and forensics people are crawling all over the place. But so far we can't tell that she was ever there." He cleared his throat. "We think that the robbers got out of Albuquerque quickly, drove up to the Davies place, hid the truck and may have switched vehicles with Melinda Davies. We're tracking down that registration so we'll soon know what we're looking for."

"Should we come—?"

"Won't do any good," Kingston said. "We're doing all we can. And don't fly out to Romeroville. You wouldn't be allowed to land or set foot on the property."

Damn. It was as if Kingston had read his intentions.

"Drake, just sit tight. We're doing all we can. You're already getting more information than most families do in these situations."

He sighed and forced himself not to come back with an angry comment. It would do more harm than good at this point.

"Thanks, Cliff. Just, please, keep me posted. We're worried here."

"I know. I will." The call clicked off.

Ham and eggs had never tasted so bland. Drake knew they were probably fine; it was just that his taste buds, along with every other part of him, had gone dead. He and Ron sat across from each other, hardly talking. The only subject on their minds was something they really couldn't discuss at length in such a public place. Not that either of them felt like talking anyway. So, he chewed his food and kept his thoughts bottled inside.

Ron got the check and they walked back out to Drake's truck.

"So, now what?" he asked as Ron opened the passenger door.

"Sitting around the office is going to drive me crazy," Ron admitted. "And Kingston was right—if we head into the midst of their crime scene we'll cause trouble."

"I'd rather see if we can wait around at APD than to just sit home," Drake said. "Think they'd let us in?"

"Worth a try. Worst they can do is say no, send us home and we're back where we are now."

Drake drove the route that was beginning to feel too familiar and parked close to the same spot he'd taken last night. They rode up in the same elevator and went through the same security procedure before stopping at the same reception desk to ask if Detective Gonzales was in.

Gonzales's golden brown skin seemed unreasonably fresh when he stepped out to greet them. He gave pretty much the identical advice as Kingston and he showed obvious reluctance to let them come back to the squad room. Ron was about to turn around, and Drake was about to argue when a man came rushing in.

He was a thirty-something guy with curly dark hair that looked a little like a floor-mop, handsome in that California way, smooth skinned, purposely dressed-down in scruffy jeans and a ripped T-shirt. Drake had seen a dozen just like him on various movie jobs. The guy looked around, obviously trying to figure out if he was in the right place. The officer at the desk asked how he might help, and Drake noticed that Gonzales was listening. Gonzales's awareness of the newcomer had the effect of drawing everyone's attention that direction.

"—ransom demand," the man was saying.

Gonzales stepped over and asked the guy to repeat.

"I'm a producer. We're doing the new Cristina Cross film." He paused as if he either wanted an oohh out of them or just to be sure they were up with him so far. "I got a call awhile ago from some nut job who says he's holding Cristina hostage and wants a five million dollar ransom for me to get her back. It's so weird that I thought you guys should know about it."

Dave Gonzales raised an index finger to get the producer to hold on. "Just a second." He directed the desk officer to page Cliff Kingston, who came hustling out of the squad room a few seconds later.

Kingston pulled out his FBI badge. "Kidnappings are usually our department."

"Good, FBI . . . See, that's the thing. Cristina has not been kidnapped. I just talked to her, like ten minutes ago."

Chapter 14

"Domino! You dumbass!" String's greeting woke me from the restless sleep I'd finally allowed myself.

I muttered a little and rolled to my back, the better to observe through nearly-closed eyelids. I still wanted the gang to think that the sleeping pill had worked.

String batted Billy on the side of the head, bringing the younger man out of his sound sleep. Billy leaped to his feet, as if that would prove he hadn't really been asleep on the job, but he swayed unsteadily for a second.

"Get in the kitchen and whip us up some eggs or somethin'."

Billy found his footing and followed along silently. The rest of them treated him like a short-order cook, placing their orders. I heard pans clattering and got a whiff of the gas range being lit again. Soon, I could smell bacon and coffee. My stomach growled.

What to do? I needed strength but couldn't risk eating anything they gave me. I stayed still for the moment, a good thing because String and Kid came into the living room, nearly catching me with my eyes open. I slammed them shut and listened.

"Put the batteries in this thing," String said.

I heard the crisp sounds of plastic packaging materials. A sly peek revealed Kid kneeling at the coffee table, not four feet from me, fiddling with a package that appeared to contain a small radio.

String, sitting in the armchair where Billy had slept, was slicing open one of those deadly-tough plastic packs, attempting to get a pair of flashlights out of it. A bulk pack of D-cell batteries rested on his lap.

"Breakfast!" Billy called out.

"Bring it in here," String ordered. "Think I got time to drop what I'm doing for you?"

Billy showed up in the doorway with two paper plates loaded with eggs, bacon and toast. He placed one on the arm of String's chair and set the other on the coffee table. "There you go, Ollie."

My stomach growled again. I covered by rolling to my side once more. "Think I should make some eggs for her?" Billy asked, nodding my direction.

String studied me for a few seconds. "Nah, ain't worth waking her up for."

Now I had to pretend to be asleep while the smells of freshly cooked food wafted around me. If I can bluff my way through this, I'll have your Oscar, Cristina Cross!

"Besides, we got stuff to talk about that's best kept just between us. You sure she's sound asleep?"

"Oh yeah, String. You shoulda seen her conk out just a few minutes after she took that pill."

"Okay, good. Get Mole and come in here to eat."

I gave a soft little snore, just to make it convincing. I love eavesdropping.

Once Billy and Mole had found places to sit, String started talking. "I figure we better give the guy at least until Monday morning to get the money. He'll have to call a bank or somethin' to come up with five mil."

Whoa. Nice that they thought I was worth five million. But I made sure no hint of a smile appeared on my face. I wondered if these jokers had any clue that it would take a good-sized truck to deliver five million dollars in cash. Well, I wasn't going to be the one to burst their bubble.

"What'd you tell him?" Billy asked.

"You shoulda seen me. Just like in the movies. I didn't let him talk, just spelled out what we wanted and hung up before anybody could run a trace on the phone."

As if this producer could possibly be expecting the need to trace the call. I peered through my lashes but kept my mouth shut.

"I just told him to get the money together and wait for my instructions." His lip curled, even more than normal. "I thought I handled it pretty well."

"Yeah, except for using your own cell phone," Mole said.

String glared at him. Bad move, spoiling the boss's story.

"I took care of that," String said.

Billy was looking at him curiously. Ollie piped up. "No big deal. Bought another, one of them throwaways."

"Did you ditch the old one?" Billy asked. "Cause I saw

on *CSI* how they can track you with a GPS from your cell phone's card."

"I thought of that," Mole said. "We dumped it in the trash, right there at the Wal-mart."

"When will we get our shares?" Ollie asked.

"Don't worry about it," String said. "I've got a place we can go, divide it up. Then we split off in different directions."

"Your house in Albuquerque?" Billy asked.

"No, stupid. This place can't be traced to me. And, trust me, the cops don't want to get near it. I can send the whole joint sky high if I want."

Mole's eyes glittered dangerously at this news but the younger guys went quiet. I kept my eyes shut while they cleared the remains of the meal. The whole group went into the kitchen, convinced that I was indeed out of it, enough that they didn't need to keep a guard posted beside me. Someone went out the back door and came back. Chairs scraped as they repositioned themselves around the table.

With breakfast finished, I wondered how they planned to keep occupied for a day and a half, until they could call the producer again. Of course, only I knew that they had the wrong hostage and there would be no five million coming. I had to work on a means of escape, quickly, before they learned that the real Cristina was not the woman in this room.

As it turned out, quibbling over the bank money occupied most of the afternoon, with the four of them gathered at the kitchen table. The counting process had been so confusing last night that no one had a clue how much each robber was supposed to have. And now that Ollie had turned up, they had to appease him, or at least make all the right noises to let him think he was getting a share.

I still didn't put it past String and Mole to get rid of the other two and keep it all. For that matter, if it came down to a shoot-out between those two bad guys I wouldn't be at all sure where to place my bet, especially since a bottle of whiskey had been added to the mix somewhere around mid-afternoon.

At some point String called out for dinner, which by the sounds of things was going to be baloney sandwiches. Billy was pressed into service once again to provide the food—a job at a pizza place apparently gave him a lot more in the way of credentials than I ever would have imagined. I heard him grumble a little bit about having to wait on them, but by the noises coming from the kitchen it sounded like he complied anyway.

My eyes had been wide open for some time now and when it became impossible to lie in the same position for another minute, I twisted myself around on the saggy sofa until I was sitting up. My head felt fuzzy from all the inactivity and I chided myself about becoming too complacent. The one thing I could not rely on was this bunch letting their guard down. If I were to escape I needed a more specific plan.

I was sitting there with my thick head in my hands when I sensed motion.

"You hungry, Miss Cross?" It was Billy.

I shrugged a 'not really' signal. I was so famished that even a baloney sandwich sounded good, but I couldn't take the chance that String wouldn't grind up another pill and sprinkle it into the mayo.

"I need to move around. Couldn't I have my legs free for awhile?"

String had moved into the doorway, staring at me, watching to see if Billy slipped me an unauthorized sandwich or something.

Billy glanced at the boss.

String eyed me.

"You try a move like last night, I'll make you sorry." He tilted his head toward Billy. "Cut her legs loose. Don't let her out of your sight."

That order resulted in another really embarrassing trip to the bathroom, but I figured if I lived through the weekend I could live through a little embarrassment.

In the kitchen the men sat around the table with a card game in progress; the radio on the countertop blasted away with country music. The whiskey bottle was more than half empty—or less than half full, if that made me sound more optimistic. I stood to the side, with Billy's eyes never leaving me. Guess the guy took String's orders seriously.

On the counter sat the remains of a loaf of bread and what was left of the baloney. My stomach growled ferociously.

"Mind if I make myself a sandwich?" I asked. I kind of said it quietly and directed the request to Billy, hoping not to make an issue of it.

He glanced at String and the older guy gave the nod. With my awkward, duct-taped grip, I pulled two slices of bread from the wrapper and two slices of meat from the plastic package. No spread, even though I doubted they'd tainted it. Even plain, it tasted good to me. That sandwich went down so well that I helped myself to a second one during a moment when the poker play got especially heated.

My energy began to return and I reminded myself not

to get so run down again. I needed physical strength as well as mental acuity when it came time to make my break. The four-against-one odds weren't good, and I had no idea what I faced once I got outside the house.

From the windows I only got glimpses of wide fields that had once been under cultivation but were now fallow. The short weeds wouldn't really count as protective foliage if I made a run for it.

The men were so wrapped up in their game that they paid little attention to me, but I remembered my experience from last night and this time I was clear across the room from the door. Realistically, there was no way I could make a dash for it. The living room had a door leading outside, but String had moved a heavy cabinet against it on the chance that I might try that while I was supposedly asleep on the couch. I might give the thing a shove, but not quietly. As long as they were in the house, I was stuck here too.

I became more fully aware of the radio when the music stopped and a news broadcast began. It started with national news, something about tax protests in Washington, but I envisioned the announcer switching to regional happenings and realized it was entirely possible that the bank robbery and my kidnapping might be a story.

A story that would name me for who I really was.

And that just couldn't happen right now.

I edged toward the sink, as if I were going to wash up, but my hands, big and clumsy with all that duct tape, swung around at the wrong moment and the poor little radio went soaring. It crashed against the stove with bits of plastic flying everywhere. And it went blessedly silent.

In fact, the whole room went silent. Four sets of unfriendly eyes stared at me.

Oscar time again. "Oh! My god!! I'm *so* sorry!" I raised my hands to my face, worked up a couple of tears. Repeated the 'so sorry' part about a dozen more times.

Mole let loose with some choice words. String looked ready to punch something. The two younger guys seemed stunned. Eventually, though, Ollie stood up for me.

"Hey, it wasn't her fault," he said. "It was sittin' kinda near the edge."

This resulted in a shouted version of the blame-game, where no one wanted to take the rap for setting the radio too near the edge of the counter. At least the attention was no longer on me.

I settled into my familiar corner of the floor since there were no more chairs and gloated in my small triumph. At this point I'd take any little victory I could grab because the alternative was to start thinking of home and Drake and wondering what was going on. Were they looking for me? Did they have any leads?

I knew I couldn't count on a rescue. Drake would be here in a flash if he knew where I was, but I just didn't see how that could be possible. No, I would have to work my own way out of this mess.

Chapter 15

The producer pulled a photo from the leather over-shoulder bag he carried. Cristina Cross could be Charlie's sister. Drake felt a pain jab through his heart.

Kingston kept his cool. "What, exactly, did you say to the caller?"

The producer, who introduced himself as Darren Stein (although it was spelled DeRon on his business card), had followed Kingston to the squad room, with Drake and Ron trailing along.

"I guess I just sputtered some nonsense," Stein said. "The demand completely took me by surprise. We've finished shooting Cristina's parts in the film and she took a couple weeks off to visit an aunt in London. The crew's just here wrapping up the second unit footage."

Kingston by now had everyone seated at a table and he was making notes on a small notepad. He'd gotten the basics about what time the call came in and the fact that the number came up as anonymous on Stein's cell phone.

"The guy rattled off a demand, said he'd call again and that I better have the money ready to deliver. He hung up so fast I was still standing there with my mouth open."

He shifted in his seat, looking like he wished he'd not gotten tied up in all the hoopla.

Welcome to the club, thought Drake. How many times had he wondered what he'd be doing right now if Charlie had only arrived at the bank fifteen minutes later.

"Look, I don't know how I can help," Stein said. "Cristina's a nice girl, really a sweetie to work with, you know. But there's no way she's worth five million dollars to the studio. She's had one TV series, a half dozen bit parts in films. The one we're doing now is probably her biggest and it's just a supporting role. She shows up in *People* often enough because she's got a good publicist." He shrugged. "I'd like to help you out here but it's gonna come out pretty soon that she's alive and well in London."

Kingston set his pen down and clasped his hands in front of him. "That can't happen."

The Hollywood guy looked like he wanted to play some kind of importance game but at Kingston's stern gaze he settled back into his seat.

"We're not asking you to come up with the money. The Bureau knows how to handle those things. We're just asking that you contact Miss Cross and tell her to stay put in London, to stay low-key, and to keep her publicist from releasing any stories about her being there."

"She's promot—"

"It's a request at this point, Mr. Stein, but it would only

take a word from me to have you detained and to round up that publicist and tie up a whole lot of his or her time, as well. And Miss Cross might find it somewhat uncomfortable to be extradited in cuffs and held in an underground interrogation room somewhere. You described her as a 'sweetie' I think. So I'm guessing that a bad-girl image really doesn't fit, huh?" He stared at the producer until the younger guy blinked.

"It's only for a few days, Mr. Stein. These bad dudes want their money quickly. They'll call back any time now, we'll stage a drop for the money, get our hostage out of their hands . . . You'll go back to making your movie and your little star can show up and pose for the cameras all she wants. Are we good with that?"

"What do I have to do?" Stein asked, barely masking the twitch of impatience that flicked across his mouth.

"I can keep you almost entirely out of it if you'll work with me."

Stein nodded.

"How well-known are you? I mean, your face, your voice. You do a lot of interviews, or those extras on DVDs, that talking-head stuff?"

DeRon didn't want to admit that he wasn't quite that important. He shrugged nonchalantly. "Not much, some."

"I'm thinking one of us can pose as you to handle all the contact work. If there's no chance that the robbers would know they're being scammed, we can keep you totally out of it."

Drake couldn't stop himself. "Hey, they think Charlie is this Cross woman. They can't be all that up on their Hollywood trivia."

He received a nod from Kingston and a glower from Stein.

"Okay," said Kingston. "I'm pretty good with voices. You said you didn't speak much during the ransom call?"

"That's right."

Kingston repeated Stein's last few comments, doing a credible job of imitating the younger man's voice.

"We'll need his cell phone, won't we?" Gonzales asked. "It's probably the only number the perps have."

Stein acted like they'd asked for his right leg. He sputtered about all his contacts and how many calls he took each day.

"Get a technician on it," Kingston suggested. "We can probably clone the number, monitor everything and pass along the non-related calls."

Stein screamed 'lawyer' until Kingston informed him that if he wanted it that way, the phone was now being seized as material evidence. The producer calmed down and grumbled that he supposed he could work with them.

"Come with me," Kingston said. "I want to record your voice so I can practice it."

Drake and Ron watched as Stein followed the FBI agent off to another room. The photo of Cristina Cross still lay on the table.

"Strong resemblance," Dave Gonzales said.

"Uncanny," Ron agreed.

Drake stared at it. Cross was a glossier version of Charlie, who almost never wore makeup and was more likely to have her long hair up in a ponytail than those waves that fell around Cross's shoulders. But the shape of the face, hair color, eye color—yes, it was a little too close for comfort.

He paced over to the windows, stared out. Hours had passed since he woke up this morning and he felt almost no closer to finding Charlie. The sun was already past the midday point.

His attention was drawn back to the table when Kingston returned. Ron had brought along the printouts he'd done from the internet pages of Melinda Davies, and he was in the midst of going over again with Kingston the relationships he'd figured out.

Kingston pulled a mug shot from the folder in front of him, a folder, Drake noticed, that seemed to be getting thicker by the hour.

"Leon Mohler. I recognize him," Ron said.

"Right. Bad dude. Lot of drug and prostitution busts on his sheet."

Drake felt himself go cold. Again, the urge to dash off, to simply get out there and do *something*. He stared out across the city.

A few minutes passed—or maybe an hour—the low hum of background noises barely registering until a familiar voice intruded.

"Cliff, got a second?" It was Dave Gonzales. Standing beside him, a young officer in jeans and an APD T-shirt. Above the pocket: Simpson, Crime Lab.

"This is Mitch from the lab. He's our best techie on site and he's got a break for us."

The mood at the table went up by about twelve beats. Drake stepped over to the table where Ron sat with Cliff Kingston.

"Uh, yeah," said Mitch Simpson. "Well, I cloned Mr. Stein's phone like you asked. And Detective Gonzales asked me to look at the call that came in this morning and get as much data about it as I could? So, anyway, the phone records show the number the call came from. That's common, even though the number didn't register on the caller ID because this number isn't in Mr. Stein's contact list?"

Kingston looked a little impatient. Drake felt like shaking the young guy to speed up the explanation.

"Uh, okay, so this is the number and the name of the phone's owner."

"Leon Stringer," said Kingston. "I figured as much." He looked at the note Mitch handed him.

"The best news is that with a little more data I was able to find out the location—"

"Bottom line!" Kingston probably didn't mean to shout but his voice came out pretty strong.

"In or near Alamosa, Colorado."

"What? That's a surprise."

Clearly, what the FBI man didn't want to say was that they'd had no clue the gang could have gotten so far away.

"Do we know where in Alamosa?"

"Can't really say, sir. It's a small town and I haven't been able to narrow the grid just yet."

"Keep trying. Pinpoint it as closely as you can, Mitch."

"Yessir."

"I'm flying up there," Drake said.

"Not yet, you aren't." Kingston stood up and Drake had a momentary flash of the heavier agent trying to take him down.

"It's where they were this morning. I can be there in a little more than an hour."

"And then what? You've got a town with a population of—I don't know—several thousand folks. A lot of motels and shopping centers. You going to just hover around and hope these guys'll hear you and come out with their hands raised?"

When he said it that way, Drake realized the futility of acting on his own.

"Let's get more data. Find out if there's a connection to any of the men in the gang, some particular place they'd go to hide out. Could be they just passed through Alamosa and stopped long enough to make the phone call. Once we have more information we'll organize a team, involve local law enforcement if that seems prudent. I know what you're wanting, Drake, but we have to be organized about it. Your wife's life is literally on the line. These are bad guys and they are armed. We cannot take the chance of spooking them."

Drake felt as deflated as a day-old party balloon. He dropped to a chair.

"Look, there's not a lot you can do here," Kingston was saying. "It would be better if you go on home."

Better in what way, Drake wondered. Face an empty house where every stick of furniture in every room would remind him of Charlie? Where he'd be tempted to break into the booze and dull the pain?

"I know you're not a guy who can just sit around. You're used to being in the middle of the action. I get that." Kingston genuinely seemed regretful. "But can you see my side of it too? I can't let you endanger yourself or your wife. I'm afraid that's an order. If you do something on your own, you will be arrested for interfering with an ongoing investigation."

Ron stepped over and placed a gentle hand on his shoulder. "Let's get out for awhile. Get some fresh air or something."

"I need to be here. If another ransom call comes in—"

"We'll call you," Kingston said.

"But I need to see her. Make them send a picture showing that she's okay. I need to see that."

"We will. We need to see that too. Meanwhile, I'm making

arrangements for some cash. These guys obviously have no clue that five million dollars won't fit into some kind of bag they can carry. But we'll come up with something convincing enough to get their attention. When the moment comes, we want the bait ready."

"Drake—" Ron's voice was quiet, thoughtful. He turned to Kingston. "We'll come back later, if that's okay?"

The agent nodded.

Drake had the distinct impression that the police and FBI would rather that he stayed completely away, just waiting at home for a call. But at least they realized *that* wasn't going to happen.

Down in the parking garage, Ron took charge. "Give me your keys, man. You're too upset to drive."

It was true but Drake drew himself up. "I manage to stay in control of an aircraft, even when there's fire below me, injured people in the back, and my own life at stake. I can handle the truck. Just tell me where you want to go."

Ron gave him a tentative smile, the first either of them had managed all day. "We may not be able to run up to Alamosa, and we may not be able to tell the police how to do their jobs, but we can still be doing something. Let's grab a burger or something and go back to the office."

Darkness fell as they finished eating. Drake sat in Ron's office watching his brother-in-law click away with his computer mouse. He'd taken the time to call their brother Paul in Phoenix and let him know the situation, cautioning him about letting any details get outside the family. If the story were to somehow get on the news . . . He thought of making a similar call to Elsa Higgins; their neighbor, closest person to a grandparent to Charlie, would be frantic if she knew . . . No, it was better to keep her out of it for now.

Better to be able to deliver some good news later on.

"I'll bet this is our place," Ron said, interrupting Drake's thoughts. "Take a look."

He had a map up on his screen, a place with the tag Stringer Farms on it.

Chapter 16

I must have drifted off because the next thing I knew I received a little nudge to my rear end.

"Hey, princess. Time to go to bed."

I looked up, dreading the implications of what that might mean. But it was Billy standing near me. String stood near the table, taking a slug from the whiskey bottle, finishing it off. Ollie appeared to be stacking the deck of cards, watching String warily.

Billy reached down and put a hand under my elbow to give me a boost to my feet. I felt like an ancient old woman, unable to move and creaking like a rusted hinge when I tried.

"Give her this," said String, pulling out the pill bottle again. "She can sleep on the couch. Kid, you watch her tonight."

He sent his trademark evil stare toward Billy, punishment,

I guessed, for having fallen asleep on the job earlier. Ollie followed String to the living room door, probably so he could lay claim to the armchair before someone else got it.

Billy handed me my pill and I reminded him that I needed water. The second he turned his back I made sure the others weren't facing me and jammed the pill out of sight, into the pocket with the others.

Billy handed me the glass and watched my credible act as I tipped my empty hand toward my mouth and took a long drink of the water.

Ollie waited in the living room, sprawled out on the armchair.

"String says for you to go upstairs," he said to Billy. "Guess there's a coupla bedrooms."

Billy left me near the sofa and walked to the stairs that I'd noticed near the front door.

"Wait, help me with this," Ollie said. He held up a full new roll of duct tape.

"Please," I said. "Could you leave it off while I'm asleep? It's really hard to get comfortable with my legs stuck together like that."

String stepped out from another doorway, behind Ollie's chair. "Forget it. I heard that. Tape her up."

Billy gave me an apologetic look after String disappeared into the downstairs bedroom. Ollie seemed like the kind of guy who didn't much analyze things—he simply followed orders. I'd noticed that when he was around the other men he puffed up and tried hard to be one of them. But he visibly relaxed whenever String and Mole were out of the room.

A long moment passed while Billy fumbled with the tape. Ollie shifted from one foot to the other, unsure how to go about asking me to sit down with my legs together. I seriously debated shoving one of them aside and making a run for the back door before they could get their act together.

But String's bedroom was between me and the kitchen, and the door stood open. I could hear him milling around in there, and the distinctive clunk of his gun being placed on a wood surface got my attention.

Before I could give my escape further consideration, Billy was kneeling beside me and had two wraps of the tape around my jean-clad legs. The sound of the tape tearing away from the roll must have reassured String that the younger guys were doing their job. He closed the bedroom door.

I leaned into the sofa's squashy cushions, not really ready to go to sleep. Billy handed me the musty robe again to use as a blanket, then he took one of the flashlights and headed up the stairs. Ollie sat in the armchair, picking up an old gardening magazine, casting it aside.

"Can't believe they got no TV here," he muttered.

"Yeah. Looks like String's grandmother didn't go for a lot of modern stuff." I shifted and pulled the robe around my shoulders.

The sweltering June temperatures in Albuquerque had not made it to this high mountain valley and I wasn't dressed for nights that dipped into the forties.

"Bet you're missing your TV and your girlfriend," I said, mindful of the door behind which String lurked, keeping my voice low. "I heard you mention her."

He nodded wistfully. "Yeah. You know. This seemed like somethin' I could do, you know, for us. Get some money so's we can get married, have a little house somewhere."

"So, how is it you got in on the uh . . . bank job? You and String good friends or something?"

"Um, kinda related. His girlfriend, my aunt Sissy." He shrugged as if that pretty well explained everything.

"Well, he must trust you a lot, giving you his car and expecting you to secure a hiding place and meet them. I mean, he didn't ask the other guys to do anything that important." Okay, Charlie, don't lay it on too thick.

Ollie scoffed. "Ha! Yeah, some hideout I got. Woulda sat there two days and here they'd be, totally different place."

I nodded as though I'd never realized how the rest of the gang tried to betray him.

"Yeah, that must have been pretty hard to—" My mouth clamped shut when the bedroom door flew open.

"Cut the chatter!" String ordered. "I gotta get me some sleep."

He stared at me for a minute, weaving just slightly on his feet, then he went back inside and closed the door again.

I gave Ollie a little conspiratorial grin and raised my eyebrows. He blew out the candle on the coffee table as I settled onto the sofa, pulling the robe over me for warmth. I lay there with my eyes wide open.

Only in the darkness could I allow myself to think of home and Drake and Elsa and Ron and how much I missed having a dog. It had been two long months without our old retriever and the ache still would not leave my heart. Tears leaked out and ran down the sides of my face but I refused to sniffle, knowing that Ollie was over there, awake and listening to me. I rolled to my side and dabbed at my cheeks with the old woman's robe.

I swore there was no way I would fall asleep; I'd spent way too much inactive time these past two days. At some point, though, I guess I did because when String burst back into the room it shocked me awake.

Flashlight beams sliced the air, waving in crazy patterns and bouncing off the walls.

"Get everybody up!" String ordered, smacking Ollie in the shoulder.

I wasn't sure if my guard had drifted off or not, but he sure bounded out of the chair now. I drew the old robe tighter around me, watchful of String's erratic movements. He ducked back into the bedroom and came out with his pillowcase of cash, sticking his pistol into the waistband of his pants.

Mole led the procession down the stairs. "What's wrong with you?" he demanded.

The two younger guys kept their mouths shut.

"We're getting out of here. I got a bad feeling."

Mole looked impatient and grumpy from being awakened, and I half expected a fight between them. But he acquiesced.

"Get your shit together," String told them. "Five minutes!"

I tossed the robe aside and sat up.

"Cut the tape. She's gonna have to walk."

Ollie dug for a pocket knife and freed my legs.

Minutes later we were jammed into Melinda's little car again, String and Mole up front, me in the center of the back seat between the other two. I stared at the dashboard clock—1:13 a.m.—as the car sped off into the dark.

Chapter 17

Ron pointed at his computer screen. "I did searches around Alamosa for the names Stringer and Mohler. No hits on the latter, but there have been Stringers there for a long time. Lots of potatoes grown in that valley and I'm betting that's what Stringer Farms does."

"Some farmer organized a bank robbery and kidnapping?"

"Probably not. But you know, a guy on the run will often head for the parents, the cousins . . . somebody related. He already headed for his girlfriend's place yesterday and look where that got her."

"You think Kingston and Gonzales's guys know this yet?"

"Possibly. Or they're getting close. It only took me a little time."

"Call them?"

"Let's go back over there. See what else they may have come up with."

They walked into a squad room filled with guys in Kevlar vests with automatic weapons.

"We thought about waiting for another ransom call," said Kingston, half apologetically, "but that's probably not coming until Monday. I'm worried that twenty-four hours gives them too much time. They could do anything."

Thank goodness. Drake let the relief rush through him.

"How many are going in?" Ron asked.

Drake counted eight men suited up in SWAT gear. "I'll fly a team up."

Kingston opened his mouth in protest.

"State Police have an AStar, six guys plus pilot, maybe only four with all that gear. You'll need two ships. I'm going to be one of them." He stared at Kingston. "These guys aren't suiting up just to stay here. You're not planning on sending them up there in vans, are you?"

"Wait, wait, wait!" Ron said. "Are you seriously thinking of going in there with guns blazing? My sister is trapped with these guys."

"We're just getting ready. Stringer and his bunch won't be expecting any action until it's time for the ransom pickup. They don't have any clue that we know where they are. I had Chief Harris at Alamosa PD arrange for a fly-by with a crop duster, some kind of inconspicuous airplane, just before sunset. They confirmed two vehicles behind the farmhouse that belonged to Lonnie Stringer's grandmother. She died a few years back and the place has been sitting empty. It's got to be where they are."

Drake and Ron exchanged a glance.

"But still," Ron said. "All these guys in black outfits are going to spook them."

"We don't plan to get within sight. Just keep an eye on the place at a distance. The armed men will be set up, once the ransom location is known, ready to take down the gang and get Ms Parker back."

"How soon do we leave?" Drake asked.

Kingston sighed heavily. "There is no *we*, Drake. I can't—"

"You damn sure better include me!"

"I was about to say, I can't risk your life. However, I can use your help in getting the team up there. As long as you do exactly what I say and do not go off on your own . . ."

"What's our ETD?"

"An hour. Can you be ready?"

"Tell me where."

With clearance to land on the roof when they returned, Drake and Ron rushed down to the garage and then headed out to Double Eagle Airport to preflight the aircraft. Fifty-one minutes later they touched down on the brightly lit helipad. Ron climbed out and three black-clad men plus Kingston took seats in the JetRanger.

Drake pulled pitch and the loaded aircraft rose above the city lights. He radioed Albuquerque Center before following a bearing northward. His lighted wristwatch showed 11:58 p.m. when they touched down at Alamosa's small airport. The facility was closed for the night but Drake placed a call to the FBO and requested refueling. The voice on duty grumbled a bit but said he could accommodate them at five a.m.

When Drake protested, he got, "Look buddy, we're a dawn to dark operation. I got nobody I can send out until then. Four-thirty at the earliest."

Drake relayed the information to Kingston but the agent was surprisingly not upset.

"We're not flying within five miles of that farmhouse in the middle of the night," he said. "They'd hear us for sure. And they might do something desperate." Harm Charlie. That's what the agent's pointed look meant.

Kingston pulled out a detailed aerial photo map. "I'm sending out teams of three. Here, here, and there." He pointed to each end of the road that led past the farmhouse and a spot at the end of a long narrow lane leading up to the place. "First, though, I'm getting Harris and his men out here. We'll do a joint briefing."

While the agent turned away to make his calls, Drake checked his helicopter and then called Ron in Albuquerque to bring him up to speed.

Fifteen minutes later, two police SUVs and two unmarked, ordinary sedans drove up. Kingston, Drake and the eight SWAT team members met them outside the airport turnstile.

Chief Harris surprised Drake. He'd expected a pudgy hometown guy with political connections, the type who fell into the job and kept it forever. Harris was a hundred-eighty pounds of solid muscle, ramrod straight spine, shoulders that packed his windbreaker; he looked like he'd just finished a tour of duty driving tanks over terrorists somewhere in the Middle East. Even Kingston sucked his gut in and stood a little straighter when the lawman approached.

Harris shook hands all around and introduced the driver of the other cruiser as his second in command, Sergeant Rick Hodgkins. The other two officers waited beside the cars. "Glad to help," he said when Kingston thanked him for being there. "Lonnie Stringer was trouble from the time we were kids. Used to spend some time here in the summers. Elvira tried her best with him, took him to church, had him work the farm right along with the other hands. None of it helped. He'd sneak into town and find the bars, get the men to give him beers. Some of them thought it was cute to see a ten-year-old guzzling booze. Even when he wasn't drunk, Lonnie would pick fights with the rest of us. Like he was tougher or better because he came from the city. Some guys would take him on, most just stayed clear. Of course I haven't seen him in more than twenty years. No telling what he's like now."

"He hasn't straightened up," Kingston said.

He unfurled the map again. "Okay, men. Let's get busy." Pointing at the locations he'd shown Drake he quickly dispatched three of his team with Hodgkins to a spot two miles west of the turnoff to the Stringer place. Harris would drop two men at the driveway itself where they would stay low and concealed. Then the Chief would take the other three to wait at the east end of the farm road, where it met the main highway. They would use the unmarked cars, trying not to spook the robbers if they were to hit the road.

"There's no other way to get a vehicle away from that house, so if they make a move we'll get them."

Drake cleared his throat.

"Right." Kingston turned somber. "Remember, they have a female hostage. So far we have reason to believe that they are treating her all right—they want a ransom for her. But . . . well, just be very cautious with these guys. They've killed two women already."

Harris nodded. "It's a little after one o'clock. Let's get in place."

Drake watched the men load their gear into the two cars and climb in. He felt utterly useless as they drove off into the black night.

"Now what?" he asked Kingston.

The agent picked up the briefcase he'd brought along. "We set up a command post." He began walking toward the cruisers. "Harris has given us full access to his department."

Drake fought drowsiness during the ride into the center of town. He couldn't remember when he'd actually slept. Last night he'd dozed for awhile in Charlie's office, but the past twenty-four hours were becoming a blur. How did Kingston do this all the time?

"Sir?"

Drake realized that the young officer who'd driven them was speaking to him. The SUV had come to a stop outside a neat brick building.

"If you're tired, sir, there's a small lounge inside with a couch."

"Do it, Drake," Kingston said. "We'll do a fly-by at daybreak. I'll need you alert."

The prospect of action buoyed him, but he found that he had no trouble drifting off to sleep within minutes after stretching out on the sofa.

He woke to the clatter of porcelain. The officer they'd ridden with last night was on the far side of the small room, setting up a coffee maker and mugs.

"Sorry it wasn't a very long rest for you, sir."

"Is Kingston getting ready?"

Drake glanced at his watch and saw that it was after four.

"Yes, sir, he's in the squad room."

Drake eyed the coffee maker.

"I'll bring you both a cup when it's ready."

"Thanks." Drake stood up and stretched out the kinks in his limbs. He located the men's room and washed his face, running fingers through his hair.

Kingston stood near a window, staring down at the street one floor below, his gray hair neatly combed and his clothing relatively unrumpled. Golden street lamps softened the darkness outside. The quiet street showed no movement, but this was a farming community—people would begin their day soon.

"Figured you might want these to go," the young police officer said, raising a pair of lidded foam cups.

Kingston and Drake accepted the wake-up juice gladly. After a few sips, Drake began to feel antsy to get moving.

"I was on the phone with the men on stakeout throughout the night," Kingston told him. "No traffic at all."

"Are they planning to raid the house?" Drake asked.

"No. We'll just keep an eye on the place from a distance. Don't want to spook anyone. It's Sunday, and I'm guessing the robbers will lie low today, place another ransom call tomorrow." He pulled a cell phone from an inner pocket of his jacket and held it up. "The clone of Stein's cell. Darn thing rings constantly but Mitch rigged it up for me so I can forward his legitimate calls with one button."

He drained his coffee cup and headed toward the lounge for more. "Meanwhile," he said over his shoulder, "I want to do a recon with your aircraft. Take a look from a distance."

Drake was glad for something to do. The waiting game felt interminable. Fifteen minutes later, in a borrowed staff car, they arrived back at the airport, just in time to watch a mechanic open the doors.

"Boss said you need fuel this morning?"

"Yeah." Drake did a few quick calculations on weight, altitude and distance and told him how much to add.

They were airborne twenty minutes later, watching the sky turn from slate to pale gray. Beside him, Kingston adjusted his headset and began to dig into his briefcase. He pulled out an impressive pair of binoculars.

"High power, stabilized. If we approach on the downwind side we should be able to get a look from a half-mile away without them ever knowing we were there."

Drake checked his wind indicator and made a small course correction. Below, neat square fields filled most of the valley, which was rimmed by high peaks. To the east the sun was beginning to hit the tops of a bunch of the 14-ers, many of which still had snow at their crests. He climbed to a thousand feet above ground level, both to get the lay of the land and to mask their sound.

It only took a couple of minutes for him to spot the layout from the aerial map they'd viewed last night—the highway that ran almost due south into New Mexico, the turnoff where Kingston's men were posted. Their plain sedan sat near the intersection and he could barely make out the shape of the plain-clothed officer who stood at ease beside it. The SWAT men were undoubtedly nearby, hidden well enough that they wouldn't alert anyone who drove by.

"That's the Stringer property," Kingston said over the intercom. He pointed out the dirt lane leading to the two-story farmhouse. Even at this distance it looked forlorn.

"I'll stay to the east," Drake said. Prevailing wind came from the west. "Tell me if I need to get closer."

Kingston raised the binoculars to his eyes and took a

moment to find the house. "You're okay. Slow the airspeed a bit, if you can. I want a good long look."

Drake complied but kept his forward momentum. A helicopter hovering over one spot would be just as conspicuous as one buzzing over the rooftop. He kept the farmhouse in view, studiously observing a safe distance.

"Uhhh-ohhh." Kingston drawled the word out too long and Drake turned to look at him.

"What?"

"I'm only seeing one vehicle behind the house. Our intel yesterday said there were two, Melinda Davies's silver Toyota and Stringer's old white Pontiac. I'm only seeing the Pontiac."

"What does that mean?" Drake had a sickening feeling he knew the answer.

Kingston had his radio out and began barking questions to the units on the ground. Over the rotor noise and his own headset Drake couldn't make out their answers. He concentrated on his instruments.

"You sure?" Kingston said clearly. "Okay. I want unit two to approach the house. Come across the western edge of the field until you come to that row of windbreak trees, the pines. Skirt those and get in close. Report if you see any signs of occupation."

More static buzzing over the radio.

"We need to move off to the side but stay nearby," the agent told Drake.

Drake concentrated on making a wide circle away from the farmhouse, although everything in his gut told him to head straight there and land on the property.

Fifteen long minutes went by.

He'd cruised the better part of the town by now.

Ten more minutes. They were just about back where they'd been when Kingston's binoculars revealed the absence of the sedan.

The two-way erupted in static again. Drake strained to hear what they were saying.

Chapter 18

Just tell me where we're going, String. I can find the place."
Mole sounded impatient with the whole dead-of-night relocation.

I couldn't say that I didn't feel the same. What had possessed String to make the sudden move? At ten o'clock I would have sworn he'd had enough whiskey to keep him out for hours. Now here we were, at two o'clock in the morning on some pitch-black Colorado road.

"Shut up! I'll let you know." String's voice sounded ragged and desperate.

I slid my gaze toward Billy, who appeared just about as freaked as I. Ollie, to my left, looked like a kid who must have done this before. I pictured him maybe with deadbeat parents who skipped out a jump ahead of the landlord/repo man/loan shark—whatever the occasion demanded. He'd nestled into his corner of the car, watching String through half-lidded eyes, the kind of teenager who would spring like a jumpy cat the second things went wrong.

"Take a left, next junction," String said. He lowered his visor and stared at his face in the vanity mirror, running a hand over the heavy stubble. Then he caught me looking at him.

"Blindfold her." The venomous tone made everyone pay attention.

Billy froze for a second.

"Now!"

Billy rummaged around, coming up with a scarf of some kind that Melinda must have left on the little shelf behind the back seats. I didn't have much choice but to let him tie it around my face. I'd noted enough signs to know that we were headed west but the left turn Mole took just before my vision disappeared would put us southbound again, back toward New Mexico.

"Sorry," Billy whispered.

"It's okay. I'm sleepy anyway." Actually, not. My nerve endings had never felt quite so raw. Almost made me wish I really had swallowed the sleeping pill.

I edged down in my seat and pretended to sleep, hoping to pick up clues as they talked. But conversation lagged after just a few minutes and no further directions seemed to be forthcoming, so I found a semi-comfortable position with my chin dropping toward my chest and eventually dozed a bit to the hum of the car and rush of tires against the road.

Voices intruded into my consciousness, little scraps of conversation, and I snapped awake, realizing with horror that I'd leaned over and was resting my head on Ollie's shoulder.

"—little burg up here soon," String was saying. "We'll get some breakfast."

"What about—" Mole's voice. A brush of fabric on fabric. "Somebody might see that we got a girl with a blindfold."

"Yeah. We'll take it off, we see anyone around."

I shifted, hoping that it looked like I was just stirring in my sleep.

"Not like she could call somebody and tell 'em where we are." Mole chuckled a little at the suggestion.

"Never know," came String's comment. "Here's the place. Not much. Little convenience store. Pull around kinda to the side. Kid, you run in and get us some donuts." He turned in the seat as Mole parked. "And coffee."

Coffee. And even a packaged donut would taste like a sliver of heaven. I nearly drooled inside my blindfold.

Apparently there were no people milling around. No one made a move to take the scarf off my face. It occurred to me that the main reason String wouldn't let me see the little town or crossroads or whatever it was, was because I would see something that could identify the place. The knowledge made me itch to snatch off the blindfold and have a good look around, but about the time I worked up the nerve to try it Ollie came back.

He tapped at the glass and Mole slid his window down.

"Hey, it's hard to fit five cups into one of these little carrier things. It's only made for four."

Bless him, he'd included me.

String muttered something. I smiled, having no clue whether Ollie could see me or not.

Ollie's side door opened and closed again. The car started. The interior became filled with the sounds and

motions of a paper bag being passed around. We began
moving, with a few choice words flying as the car hit ruts
getting back onto the road.

Tempers settled once we were on smooth pavement
again but the smell of coffee and donuts was driving me
crazy. I reached up with my clumsy double hands and
pushed the blindfold upward. The horizon was visible to
our left, with a pale gray sky beginning to reveal itself.

String seemed busy stuffing his face. I turned toward
Billy and gave him a look that said, Hey! He pulled the last
cup of coffee from the cardboard carrier and handed it to
me. Although I normally do a little routine with cream and
sugar, today it didn't matter. The pure black liquid tasted
great, just the way it was. No wonder I'd felt so lethargic—
two whole days without this. I let the caffeine rush straight
to my brain.

I needed that.

It was time, I decided, to stop being quite such the quiet
little thing, the go-along-with-the-group sweetheart. They
thought I was some Hollywood celeb, well, let them start
treating me like one.

"Got any chocolate ones left?" I said, nodding toward
the paper bag that sat on the console between Mole and
String.

Ollie reached for it and offered the open sack toward
me. I could just see myself holding a donut with both hands
and scarfing at it like a starving ragamuffin.

I raised my taped wrists. "This is ridiculous. I can't reach
for everything two-handed. You've kept me this way for two
days and the tape is gross and disgusting." It was true. The
adhesive was beginning to blacken and my skin felt like it
wanted to separate from my bones.

String caught the little outburst and turned in his seat to stare at me. Billy looked at the boss with utter trepidation.

"Okay, yeah. Give her a little break," String said. "But you two watch her. I don't want no trouble from the little bitch."

Billy pulled out his little pocket knife and sliced the tape. It peeled off with a *rrrippp* that left raw patches. I gasped and grabbed at the tender skin.

After a minute or so I took a donut and then a second one.

The combination of sugar, fat and caffeine worked magic as a quick energy boost, but I had to wonder if these guys ate this way all the time. Hey, I'm no junk food prude; I love all this stuff. But where was the protein? And even I crave a salad and some veggies from time to time.

The moment would come when I needed to make a move to get myself out of here and I couldn't see doing it on donut power alone. Unfortunately, it didn't seem that I had much choice in the matter.

"Hey, if there's a kitchen wherever we stop tonight, I'll cook for you guys." Now where had *that* come from? I *don't* love to cook, even under the best of conditions.

String turned slowly to face me. "You what?"

"Uh . . . well . . . I mean, I can make stuff. You know, maybe some pasta or um . . . something. I can cook chicken, stuff like that."

String looked at me like I'd come from another planet. Billy and Ollie both had wistful stares, like maybe their dream mom had just showed up.

I drew myself up a bit and tried to think like a movie star would. "Well, not that I really allow myself much of that food anymore. My personal trainer has me on salads, low fat, high fiber main dishes . . . you know."

Since I didn't have a clue about what a personal trainer would actually recommend I figured I better shut up.

"You make your own food at home?" String clearly couldn't grasp the concept. "You don't eat out in fancy restaurants all the time?"

Geez, how would I know? I needed to get more adept at this role they'd put me into. It hit me that I knew nothing about Cristina Cross and if any of these guys did, I would quickly blow my chances. Was she married? Did she have children? Did she actually live in Hollywood? She might be one of those Hollywood-to-Santa Fe transplants, for all I knew.

"Just offering," I said, sinking back down into my small wedge of seat space.

No one spoke for another twenty miles, until String gave Mole instructions to turn west. By my calculation (and by the condition of the road) I was pretty sure that we'd crossed back into New Mexico around daybreak. If we were now heading west we might be approaching the Four Corners area. Names of small towns showed up occasionally on signs but I wasn't familiar with them, especially the unpronounceable Navajo ones. I picked some adhesive residue off the back of my left hand, mainly for something to do.

I occupied my mind with calculations. I know, it's a weird accountant thing.

Starting with the big stuff, it was now almost exactly two days since my badly timed visit to the bank. That was Friday, so this must be Sunday. I suppose any first-grader could have figured that one out.

My one ill-advised attempt to scramble out the door

had only backfired, giving the men all the more reason to keep me taped, doped and blindfolded, and it seemed that every one of my plans for other ways to get out of this mess had been thwarted. An image of Snidely Whiplash saying "curses, foiled again!" came into my head and I knew I'd definitely taken a mental turn for the worse.

Chapter 19

Kingston pointed toward the farm and Drake gave it some right pedal. Less than two minutes later he spotted a wide, clear spot between the house and a large silo out back. The sun cleared the distant peaks and hit the roof of the decaying house just as he landed the ship there.

From the trees and nearby fields, men in black swarmed the place. Kingston climbed out, gun drawn. "Stay here," he ordered.

Drake left the rotors in motion, tightened the friction on the collective and on the cyclic, then reached for the pistol he'd brought along. He wanted to leap out and rush into that house, frustrated at Kingston's warning not to get in the way. His chest constricted, hoping against hope that Charlie would be there, that maybe the robbers had left her behind and fled to save their own skins.

Shouts of "Clear! Clear!" echoed from the wooden

structure within minutes of the onslaught.

A man came out the back door, shaking his head. "Nobody here," he called out to Kingston. Drake took his hand off the grip of his pistol and left it in his jacket.

The FBI man waved Drake over. The black-clad agent walked toward them.

"They were here," he said. "There's food in the kitchen, beds look slept in, but they've gone."

"Let's take a look. See if we can get an idea how long ago," Kingston said. He turned to Drake. "You might be of help, spot something. But do not touch or disturb anything inside that house. Until we have a chance to go over it, anything at all might be evidence."

Drake nodded. Knowing he was this close to Charlie, he would agree to anything. He shut down the ship and followed Kingston across the dirt yard, past a junker white Pontiac and onto the home's small wooden back porch.

At its best, the plain farmhouse had been utilitarian. An old chrome and linoleum table and chairs filled most of the kitchen floor space. A faint odor of gas indicated that the stove had been used recently. The counter tops were littered with packages—bread, crackers, half a jar of peanut butter, an empty whiskey bottle, a package of lunchmeat that was beginning to reek without refrigeration in the summer heat. Burned-down candles had dripped wax on table and counters.

"No power," Kingston commented, flipping a light switch. "Probably cut off, way back when the old woman died."

"Two bedrooms upstairs," reported one of the agents. "Lots of old furniture but it looks like the rooms were mainly used for storage."

"Bathroom on the ground level was used and it's really rank. I closed the door. One bedroom down here," said another man. "Looks recently used. It seems the best furnished of them all."

Kingston and Drake headed through a door into a living room, then into the bedroom. A full-size bed held rumpled heaps of bedding, mostly homemade quilts in multi-colored patterns. A candle had burned down to nearly nothing, leaving a heap of wax on the nightstand. A dresser across the room held a couple of framed family photos, things that dated back to the 1940s by the look of them.

Back in the living room, a heavy cabinet lay on its side, obviously tipped over when the agents had kicked through the front door. A sagging brown sofa and smashed throw pillows indicated that someone must have slept there. A thin pink bathrobe lay in a heap beside the nearby coffee table. The room's other furnishings consisted of a classic woodstove that some antique dealer would probably love to get his hands on, plus an overstuffed green armchair and a smaller, upright one with a flowered slipcover. A little shelf unit, the kind that used to be given as bonuses by encyclopedia salesmen, contained a stack of gardening magazines, an old postcard of the Eiffel Tower on a tiny metal easel and a pair of chipped ceramic kittens.

Drake glanced over it all but only one item caught his attention. A little bunched-up piece of fabric, the same color as the shirt Charlie had been wearing Friday morning. He pointed it out to Kingston and the agent picked it up.

"She wears those things around her hair, you know, a ponytail thing. I don't know what they're called." Drake's voice caught. He cleared his throat. "This is the one she wore on Friday. It matches her shirt."

Kingston handed it to him. "See anything else of hers?"

Drake shook his head. "Not yet."

"You can go with Sims and look at the other bedrooms."

Drake nodded and followed the other agent. The two upstairs rooms were just as the other guy had described. They'd been bedrooms at one time, with basic furnishings, no more. But in recent years they'd become the collect-all areas of the house. A sewing machine was probably the only item the old lady had used in the last ten years of her life. He glanced around but saw little evidence that anyone had spent time here, much less traces of Charlie.

Excited voices and the clomp of heavy boots downstairs attracted his attention. The agent who'd accompanied him was already on his way down and Drake followed.

". . . beauty of dye packs," one agent said.

"But just two?" Kingston questioned.

On the coffee table in the living room sat two canvas bags soaked in red. At a glance Drake might have thought blood. Four men stood staring at them. Kingston gingerly lifted an edge of one, peered inside, dropped it. Checked his fingers for stain but the dye had dried.

"At least one of the men is going to have this red all over his hands, probably some on his clothing too. Stuff doesn't wash out."

"That's good news then," Drake said.

"Yeah. Pretty hard for a guy to not get noticed. Harder still to lie his way out of his role in the robbery."

Kingston turned to one of the men. "Find a way to bag these as evidence. Careful, parts of them could still be wet."

The agent left and came back with some black garbage bags. Drake watched as they got the messy red bank bags inside without getting the dye on themselves.

"The bad news, of course," said Kingston, "is that it looks like they got away with one bag of good money. It's not here. And that gives them cash enough to go a good long way from here."

"It can't be traced?" Drake asked. "Serial numbers or something?"

Kingston's expression wasn't encouraging. "Not really. It's one thing if the branch got a shipment directly from the Federal Reserve, packets sequentially numbered. But the money in a teller's drawer usually contains a lot of used bills from customer deposits and such. Tracing the money as they spend it will be nearly impossible."

The agent turned and walked through the kitchen and went out back.

Drake followed. There didn't seem to be anything else in the house that mattered to him.

Outside, the teams were scanning the ground for other trace evidence but it didn't look like they were coming up with much.

"Checked the VIN on the Pontiac," Kingston said. "It's the one we knew was registered to Lonnie Stringer. No news there. We've bagged every removable thing from it and will have the car towed back to the crime lab in Santa Fe. Melinda Davies's debit card was in the glove box, which probably ties the men with her death. Otherwise, it looks like the car will only serve to prove a connection between Stringer and this location. We've already got the red truck, the only vehicle actually on scene at the bank so we're really just covering bases with this one."

"So now what?" Drake asked. "Any idea where they went?"

"Not a one."

Chapter 20

We'd been on the road about eight hours now, with only one stop besides the coffee and donut place this morning—some no-name place for gas, during which the men in the backseat were given guns to keep me from doing some stupid thing like shouting out that I'd been kidnapped.

String continued to give step-by-step directions to Mole. Each time, Mole became more resentful and they came close to fighting it out. I almost hoped they would. Mole might pull over to the side and the two of them duking it out would give me a chance to run. I looked out at the surrounding landscape.

Nothing but red earth and sagebrush, wavering in the blistering desert heat. The terrain varied a bit, but unless I got lucky enough that they stopped the car near one of the infrequent dry washes, there simply weren't a lot of ready hiding places. A bullet would catch up with me before I could get very far, and ducking into a culvert would only make me an easy target. Nope, this was not a good place to escape.

Not to mention that I'm not exactly up on my outdoor survival skills. My tomboy childhood has given over to the easy days of cell phones and GPS, and I realized that I'd never been faced with survival in desert heat in the summer without my cell phone and a toll-free number to call for roadside assistance. What would I do even if I did get away from my captors? I felt myself getting a little panicky at the thought.

For now, I decided, I better make the best of things. Even without air-conditioning, this crowded car and its sweaty occupants were, for the moment, my only way out of the vast open spaces all around me. I started to play around with a scenario in which Mole and String would get so worked up that they would stop the car, get out and start whaling on each other. Then Ollie and Billy would step out to either break up the fight, join in, or just be animated spectators. During all this I, in my quick-thinking way, would leap into the driver's seat and roar off, leaving all of them in the dust. Take that, creeps!

The more I thought about it, the better a plan it seemed. If only I could get all four of them out of the car at once . . . of course the little matter of leaving the keys behind and relaxing their guard on me at the same time didn't seem too likely. I slumped in my seat again, discouraged.

As if to underscore the unlikelihood of my plan, String began to relax and quit baiting Mole quite so much. He reclined in his seat and turned the radio up, catching a station that blared rap. We must be near a town. Radio stations that came in clearly would be few and far between out here. I stared out at the horizon and caught sight of a cluster of trees at our two o'clock position. Any sign of green out here could only exist if there were a river that flowed on a regular basis—rare—or if humans had planted and tended them. I scanned the road ahead but saw no signs. The blazing sun was almost directly overhead and the dashboard clock said it was 10:43.

String tapped Mole on the shoulder and pointed to the left. A half-mile later a narrow road appeared and Mole took it, carrying us away from the trees. Within minutes the radio signal faded, the rap music—for better or worse—becoming so static-filled that String switched it off.

I caught him staring into the back seat. On either side of me, the two younger men dozed. Being awakened a couple of hours into a night's sleep, it didn't take much effort to nap away the trip. I realized that although I felt wired and nowhere near sleepy, it might be in my best interests to let String think I was. I yawned and let my eyelids droop.

A few minutes later, String and Mole started talking in low voices.

". . . better to travel at night? Find a quiet place to hide in the daytime?" This from Mole.

"I thought about that. We might."

The whooshing tires on the road were the only sound for awhile.

"Not a big place though. Not on the Interstate." String talking.

"Sometimes those little places? The ones without much traffic . . . well, people remember things . . . strangers. You know? I'm just saying."

"Yeah, I know."

I got the feeling String would figure out how to make Mole's suggestion seem like his own idea. An hour passed without comment. I felt myself actually drifting toward sleep.

"California," Mole said.

My brain registered the word but sleep still pulled at me.

"That's where she lives," String said. "But that producer guy. He was in New Mexico, right? How do we know he's not still there? It's his phone number, right?"

Mole seemed to mull this over. "So . . . where will they bring the money?"

"They'll bring it wherever we tell them." String's confidence sounded a little forced, to me.

I peered through my closed lashes. Both men in the front seat sat back—relaxed, conversational. I didn't see another battle brewing just yet.

"I need some food," String said. "Next town, we'll stop."

My ears perked up at that. But when he turned to stare into the back seat, I appeared to be blissfully asleep.

The car slowed. Billy and Ollie stirred so it seemed like a legitimate time for me to do the same. We were on a main street of some little town. I saw Ocho Rio Hardware and Ocho Rio Supermarket, so I made a guess at the name of the town. A Dairy Queen appeared on the left and Mole pulled off the road, going around to the side of the building with the fewest windows. With the vehicle standing still, the midday June heat blasted into the car like a furnace.

Once again, they sent Ollie inside with instructions. This time, Billy went along to help with the fetch and carry. Alone in the car with String and Mole, the sweat on my body felt chilly. I stared them down but didn't for a second believe that either of them would cut me any slack once they found out I wasn't worth a pile of cash to them.

After a minute they both turned to face forward, watching the door through which the two younger guys had entered the fast food place. I briefly considered my chances of diving for one of the side doors and bailing out but that pistol was still sitting mere inches from String's fingertips. He beat a nervous rhythm on the center console until the other men appeared, some ten minutes later, Billy carrying two large paper sacks and Ollie with a cardboard tray full of soft drink cups.

They piled back into the rear seat of the car, closing off the small bit of fresh air I'd enjoyed in their absence. I'll tell you, four men in a hot car in the desert sun is not a pleasant experience, either for the eyes or the nose.

Ollie passed the drinks around and Billy handed out sandwiches.

"I thought you might like grilled chicken, Miss Cross," he said, handing me a foil-wrapped packet. Bless him.

The smell of warm meat and bread just about made me swoon. If I hadn't already been sitting, my knees would have buckled.

Mole got one corner of his hamburger unwrapped and a bite into his mouth before String ordered him to start moving. I looked longingly at the air-conditioned restaurant, but it was gone before I had time to get too attached to the idea.

Despite the sweaty bodies and unwashed clothing and oppressive heat, they managed to put away the food in record time. I have to admit that I voraciously went after my chicken sandwich and Coke, too. The wrappers joined the detritus of coffee cups and donut bag from the morning's repast, on the floor of the car. By tonight I figured it would be up to my knees.

I resisted the urge to neaten up. I'm not picky about eating in the car—what else does the term 'fast food' mean anyway?—but I confess to being one of those nutty types who tosses every bit of litter in the trash at the next stop. At the moment, though, I had more dire things on my mind than the neatness of a stolen car.

"Over there," String directed, pointing with his red-dyed right hand while tossing a crushed French-fry wrapper to the back. It landed in my lap and I flicked it to the floor.

What he was pointing out was a small motel, one of those not-quite-name-brand places that looked clean enough and was probably owned by Pakistanis. The parking lot only held a few cars, this being past the checkout time for most folks. I would have thought he'd wait and find a place later in the day when it would be easier to blend into the crowd. But I wasn't complaining—each window of each room had a nice square air-conditioning unit under it.

We parked beside a little fenced swimming pool that had plastic lounge chairs around it and not a scrap of shade. String peeled some cash off a wad he'd stuck into his pocket and handed it to Mole.

"Get a room."

Wait. One room?

"I want my own," I piped up in my best Cristina demeanor. Hey, if they wanted to think I was a star, I would make some effort at acting like one.

He shot me an annoyed glance. "Okay, make it two."

The small victory felt amazingly good.

Mole came out a few minutes later with some plastic key

cards in his hand. "I asked for rooms on the back side. Told the lady it looked shady over there."

"You didn't—"

"I didn't make a stink about it. She *won't* remember me."

Something about the way he said that chilled me. I rubbed my bare arms to ward off the goosebumps.

Two minutes later we'd parked outside Room 137. There was a little hubbub about who would walk next to me, which eventually String settled by stepping in and grabbing my arm in a grip that left no doubt that I would not simply shake him off and run for it. Both he and Mole had their hands near the grips of their pistols so the question was moot anyway.

We were on the back side of the U-shaped building, without another car or a maid in sight. No one would probably notice a gunshot or two.

I walked along with my best docile manners on. Surely an escape opportunity would present itself at some point.

My idea of having my own room was quickly quashed. The two rooms were adjoining and Mole made sure the connecting doors were open and would stay that way. Additionally, he assigned Billy to sleep in my second bed and Ollie to sit up and keep watch. The two men could switch places if they wished (how magnanimous) but I was never, under any circumstances, to be left alone. His exact words. It was the longest speech I'd yet heard him make.

Frankly, until the air conditioning got up to speed, I really didn't care. I chose the bed nearest the AC unit, cranked it up as cold as possible, and stretched out. The air dried the sweaty places on my clothes but my skin felt sticky. I got up and, after assuring myself that the bathroom door had a lock, I stripped down and took the quickest shower of my life.

Putting the three-day-old clothes back on wasn't the degree of refreshment I wanted, but I had to admit that I felt a whole lot better.

As if it had not otherwise occurred to them, once they saw what I'd done, my two guards took their turns at the shower as well. Too bad I couldn't suggest a shopping trip for fresh duds, but it was not to be.

I paced the room, to get a little exercise if nothing else, but String didn't like the movement. I caught him watching me through the connecting door and knew what he was about to do, even before he walked into my room.

"Take this. We're all gettin some sleep." He sneered, his pointy little teeth showing, as he held out the pill bottle and watched a single pill tip out into my hand. "Into the mouth. I'm makin sure you really take it."

I pinched the white pill between my thumb and forefinger and showed it landing on my tongue. When I turned to pick up my plastic cup of Coke, I shifted the pill to the side of my cheek. Then I drank deeply. Satisfied, he turned and went back into his own room.

Out of his sight I quickly fished out the pill but at least half of it had dissolved. Drat! I stuck the damp thing into the top of my sock moments before Ollie walked back into the room.

On one of the beds in the other room, String lay on his side with his hand on his pistol. Mole flopped down on the other bed and they were quiet.

Billy, semi-fresh from his shower, stretched out on the empty bed in my room and Ollie took the chair. Since it was the closest piece of furniture to the blessed AC unit, I suspected that was the real reason he accepted first stint at guard duty. I pushed the flowered bedspread aside, ignoring two cigarette burns and some stains that I didn't want to think about, and crawled under the sheet.

In their hurry to get away from String's grandmother's place, they'd come away without any fresh rolls of duct tape and I didn't want to give reason for someone to run to the nearest hardware store for more. I curled up, the most comfortable position I'd had in days, and once I heard snores from the other room, allowed myself to drift off to sleep.

Voices, raised in hot debate, roused me. I couldn't be sure of the time but some hours had passed. The room's blackout drapes were still drawn but I could tell it was dark outside.

"California," String said.

"New Mexico." It was Mole.

"Look, the lady lives in California. That producer lives there. The film company must be there—it's where they all are. That's where we go to get the money."

I could hear them moving around in their room. I did a little restless-sleep movement, just to get a quick peek around my own room. Ollie was still sitting in the chair, his attention alert to the other room. Billy snored loudly in the other bed, oblivious.

Mole paced by the open connecting door. He was shirtless, walking around in jeans and socks. The gaudy arm tattoos ran up his neck and almost completely covered his back, as well. He seemed agitated but I didn't see his gun.

"Okay, so let's say you're right," he said to String. "The producer has gone to California now. Where do we set up the pickup for the money?"

I noticed that he didn't say anything about exchanging me for the money.

"I know the L.A. area pretty well. We'll go scout out some places."

My muscles tensed. I knew good and well that neither Cristina Cross's family nor her producer were going to pay. She would probably get a good chuckle out of the unwarranted demand for money. They would chalk it up to the kinds of crank calls that Hollywood people must get all the time. Law enforcement in California knew nothing about me, about what had happened in a small branch bank in Albuquerque, New Mexico, about the small time crooks who now thought they could hit the jackpot. A ragged sob threatened to escape. I held it back.

"You don't know shit," Mole shouted. "You been to L.A., what, once ever? I tell you, we shoulda kept this thing in Albuquerque where we know people. We got a place to hide, people can help us out."

"Oh yeah, and then they either want a cut or they rat us out." String was on the move. Something made of glass shattered.

I glanced at Ollie again. He looked like a tightly wound coil, ready to spring out of here.

The voices from the other room went up another notch. Billy came fully awake in about two seconds.

"What's—?" he whispered.

Ollie gave a small shake of the head. He peeked outside, around the side of the drape.

I edged upward in my bed, sitting with my back against the wall-mounted headboard. String seemed to rule the gang with an iron hand, but this was the first time I'd seen serious dissention.

String appeared in the doorway. "C'mon! Now! We're gettin out of here." He came into my room and waved his pistol toward the door. "We're headin for California."

Mole showed up right behind him. "No. Albuquerque." His gun was in his hand now, too, and I could see this thing getting volatile, real easy.

Ollie, surprisingly, stepped forward. "Hey, let's all calm down. It's the middle of the night. We should think about this, make the ransom call in the morning . . ."

Mole stared at him, his coal-black eyes glittering. "You, shut up." He marched into the room and grabbed Billy by the shirt collar. "You. Get her ready to leave."

Billy stumbled over his own feet as he came around the corner of the bed where he'd been sleeping.

"*Estupido*," Mole muttered. "Where is the tape? I don't want her able to try anything."

Uh-oh.

"Um . . . I don't know where it is. I think we left it—"

"Hurry up!" String ordered. "I don't like this. Too much noise. Someone's going to show up."

As if in answer to his prophecy, the phone rang.

"Look at that. Somebody's complained to the manager." String aimed the gun at my head. "Pick it up. Tell them it's the TV and you'll turn it down."

All my plans of shouting for help the first time I got the chance to speak to *anybody* outside this group flew out the window. I repeated String's words and hung up the phone. He lowered the gun.

"Okay, now we're going to leave quietly." His voice was so low and ominous that no one said a word.

We all went slowly to the door and walked out into the night. My first rational thought was that at least it had cooled off quite a bit. Desert temperatures can easily drop thirty or forty degrees between day and night. This was one time that drastic difference felt welcome.

String took my arm and walked beside me with the gun at my ribs. Ollie and Billy fell in behind us, with Mole at the rear. I took one quick glance and then kept my eyes forward.

String walked past the faded silver sedan, which we'd left parked several rooms away. We rounded the corner of the building and across the lot before he began tugging door handles. The first unlocked vehicle was a Ford Explorer that was at least ten years old. He whipped open the back door and shoved me inside.

String took the driver's seat, settling the question of where we would be heading. Mole jumped into the back, right behind String, and held his gun on his lap. The way he stared at the back of String's head sent my stomach churning. Billy got into the other back seat, leaving Ollie to ride shotgun.

It took String about four seconds to hot-wire the vehicle and he had it in gear and out of the parking lot in under a minute. I imagined the owner in his room, sleeping through the whole thing with the whir of the AC unit blowing. He wouldn't discover the loss for at least another six hours.

From the motel parking lot, String made a right and carefully cruised down the main street of whatever little town we were in. Six blocks later, past dark businesses and sleepy motels, he came to the onramp for Interstate 40. He took the westbound lane.

Beside me, Mole just about came unglued. "What the hell—" He clenched his teeth and held his pistol to String's neck.

"What, you gonna shoot me while I'm driving seventy-five?"

"Pull over!"

String kept going.

"Stop the car." Mole's voice went deadly serious. "Now."

String faltered, only the slightest bit, but the balance of power had changed. From my place in the center of the back seat I could see the cold anger in his dark jaw.

"You're right, Mole. We need to settle this now."

He whipped to the right, jarring our teeth as he crossed the rumble strip and slewed the car to the very edge of the pavement. Beyond that, the roadway dropped off about three feet and I caught myself holding my breath. He could easily roll the high-centered SUV.

String jammed the gearshift lever into Park and whipped his door open so quickly it was as if the car had never fully come to a stop. His right hand grabbed up his pistol and he was at Mole's door in a split second.

The last place I wanted to be right now was inside that vehicle. Apparently the others all felt the same way. Ollie and Billy had opened their doors; I fumbled with my seat belt and scrambled to the right, ready to bail over Billy's lap if that's what it took.

A little slow on the move, Billy blocked the door with his bulky body in a fateful moment of indecision.

String, faster on the move than Mole, fired.

Billy's head slammed against the window as his body fell lifelessly out the open door.

Chapter 21

Drake sat in the silent JetRanger, running his fingers over the pale blue ponytail band he'd found in the farmhouse, feeling numb. Charlie had been this close. Although the burned candles were now cold, the food in the kitchen stale and rotting, he had a strong feeling that the gang were not that far away. They couldn't have left the house more than a few hours ahead of the FBI team's arrival.

His cell phone rang. A glance at the readout—Ron.

"What's happening?" Charlie's brother demanded.

"I should have called sooner—sorry. The robbers were here. With Charlie. But they got away before we arrived at daybreak."

"Had to be in the middle of the night," Ron said. "I mean, the other report said two cars were there yesterday afternoon, right?"

"Yeah. The stolen sedan is gone now."

"How did they get past—"

"No idea. Kingston's men are bagging evidence but I don't see much point. The day is getting away from us and we haven't found any clue as to where they might go next."

Ron sounded as discouraged as Drake felt.

"I feel like we're back at square one. I'd be surprised if we got another call today. Kingston's right, they'll probably wait until Monday and try to get the ransom money with as few calls as possible."

Ron groaned at the other end of the line. "Let me know what I can do here. I'll stay at the office."

Neither man had words to comfort the other.

Drake spotted Kingston walking through the lengthening shadows, toward the helicopter. The senior FBI man looked older and wearier than even a few hours ago. Drake slipped out of his seat and met the agent.

"I've put out a multi-state alert for the car," Kingston said.

"Let me fire this up and try tracking them from the air."

"Drake, it wouldn't do any good. Look at this map." Kingston unfolded the rumpled map they'd referred to last night. "Once they got off this property there were a dozen ways they could go. I figure they were at least a couple hours ahead of us. They could be back in New Mexico by now, or heading for Wyoming or Arizona or Utah. There's just no way to know."

"Do you think they ran because they knew we were getting close?"

"It's possible." Kingston shrugged. "But I don't know how. We made sure that no local lawmen approached this place. We coordinated everything, watched from a distance . . ."

"So are there *any* leads on the car, the one they stole from the dead woman?" Drake paced a few feet away, then back. "I can't just sit around here. Do you get that? I'm not the kind of guy who can wait and do nothing."

"Drake, calm down. Just what do you think you could do?"

Kingston looked patient enough to wait calmly for the apocalypse, but it wasn't his wife out there in the hands of desperate criminals.

"Every law enforcement agency in the Southwest has a description of the vehicle and the subjects. If they are on the road they will be spotted."

"And what happens when some small town cop pulls them over and Stringer comes out shooting? Or Mohler holds a gun to Charlie's head while a guy barely out of school fumbles to figure out what to do next?" Drake felt his blood pressure rise and wanted to put his fist through something.

"Listen, Drake. I can send you home right this minute and cut you out of the investigation altogether. You could be sitting in your living room right now, just praying for the phone to ring. That's what happens with most families in your situation. You think you feel helpless now? Well, it could be a whole lot worse." Kingston blew out a sharp breath and tamped down his temper. "We are doing the best that we can. We can't predict every possibility."

Drake felt the muscles in his jaw twitch. The lawman was right, of course, but it didn't make him feel a whole lot better.

"I know. I just feel so damn useless."

"In a way, we all do. I wish it was like they show in the movies. I wish I had the budget and equipment to track every movement of their vehicle. At this point I'd settle for a clue on where that vehicle is right now." He checked his watch, as if that would make something happen.

"You can stay with us if you like. I'll admit that your helicopter might come in handy when we do finally get a lead. I'm about to call in all the men. We'll stay in town tonight. We're online, we'll have access to the latest information. I've got Stein's phone, the one they'll most likely call."

It was dark by the time they finished dinner at a small diner in Alamosa. Drake hardly tasted the chicken fried steak he'd ordered, managing only a few bites. He'd noticed that his pants were already looser at the waist. He and Kingston walked back toward the motel where they'd set up a command post in one room and procured sleeping quarters for the team. The JetRanger was tied down securely at the airport, waiting for the moment she'd be needed again.

"Get a little sleep, Drake," Kingston said. He patted his pocket. "For the moment, all we can do is wait for another call. These guys think Charlie is worth a lot of money to them. They'll treat her okay, for that reason alone. They're probably more impatient than we are to get this thing going. They want to make the call and get the money."

Drake felt only marginally better. He stopped by the room where the computers were set up, with three agents monitoring everything. The guy Kingston had left in charge shook his head slowly when he spotted Drake. No news.

The agent was right. Drake should try to rest. He went

to his room and stretched out on the bed, removing only his boots, certain that he wouldn't sleep. But at least the pillow felt good and the place was quiet.

He was startled to see daylight at the window when someone knocked at the door. He leaped up too fast and got lightheaded. One of the black-clad agents stood at the door.

"What's happening?" Drake said breathlessly.

"They've found the car. Agent Kingston thought you'd want to know."

"I'm coming." He shoved his feet into his boots again, barely taking time to lace them, and ran toward the command room. Outside, the sky was the pale blue of early morning.

"Is she there?" he asked. "Is Charlie with the car?"

Kingston pursed his lips. "Afraid not. No one is."

Drake felt his elation take a dive.

"But it's a solid lead. It was at a motel near Holbrook, Arizona. Right near Interstate 40." The agent at the computer pointed to a map he'd brought up on his screen.

"From there, they could head back to Albuquerque. Do you think that's their plan?" Drake asked.

"No way to know," Kingston said. "They could also go west—Flagstaff, maybe. Maybe all the way to California. The good news is that I-40 is major. Plenty of law enforcement to keep a watch for them."

"But how? Do you know what they're driving now?"

"I've ordered that all reports of stolen or missing vehicles be reported to me. So far, we haven't heard of any, but I don't think it will take that long. I've alerted Arizona DPS and Navajo County Sheriffs Department about the situation. They're holding the abandoned car for us and a Bureau forensics team is on the way to pick it up. They'll comb through it for every scrap of evidence."

Kingston's jacket rang and he grabbed a cell phone from one of the pockets. "Okay, thanks," he said before clicking off the call.

"Sorry, thought that might be our ransom call. Other phone. Our guys have arrived and taken the Toyota into evidence."

The agent stepped toward Drake. "I've got a good feeling about this. They're starting to make mistakes. Leaving the car in a motel lot wasn't smart. We'll get more information soon."

Drake wanted to believe the agent's reassurances. It was just that so many things could go wrong along the way.

Chapter 22

My ears rang and I could still see the muzzle-flash, a floating bright spot in front of my eyes. The Explorer's interior reeked of gunpowder. I realized that my hands were over my ears. I may have screamed. It was all one of those instantaneous blurs.

I'd instinctively thrown myself down across the seat, right over the spot where Billy had been sitting moments before. Behind me, I knew String still had the pistol. I peeked, dreading that he might now be aiming it at me.

But he'd jerked Mole out of the car by the neck of his shirt and held the muzzle at the larger man's chin. String's eyes were wild with fury. Mole's whole face was squinted up tight, awaiting the inevitable.

Why he didn't fire, I'll never know. But he didn't.

He growled something through gritted teeth and shoved Mole, bouncing him off the rear quarter panel of the SUV.

He turned the gun toward Ollie who was having a true deer-in-the-headlights moment.

"You gonna try anything?" he snarled.

Ollie shook his head, without a word.

String glared at Mole once more. I couldn't see the other man's face but his stance had already become submissive.

A pair of lights appeared in the distance.

"Make sure they don't see nothin'," String ordered.

Mole rounded the back of the Explorer. Billy's body lay in a heap at the door, his legs still inside, very near my head.

Mole stooped down, as if he were checking the rear tire, until the other car roared by. I pushed myself upright, wanting more than anything to be at least a hundred miles away from here. I caught myself shaking. String was staring at me.

"Don't make a move," he said in a voice that let me know he was deadly serious.

I watched him, the way a kicked dog watches the guy wearing the heavy boots. His attention went back to the other two men.

"Get it out of sight," he said, "out there somewheres."

The 'it' I realized was Billy. I stared, horrified, as Ollie and Mole grabbed their partner's arms and legs and carried his body over the embankment.

"What! You're just going to leave him out here?" I felt disbelief surge through my chest.

"Well I ain't driving down the road with no stiff in the back seat," String said pragmatically. Another car zoomed by and he sent an evil stare toward me. "Don't worry, this heat, the vultures will be all over it by noon."

Bile rose in my throat. I closed my eyes and swallowed

hard.

The other two men came out of the darkness and got back into the SUV, Mole riding up front again. Ollie climbed into Billy's former spot. At least I didn't have to sit there with his blood on the doorjamb beside me. I edged into the seat directly behind String.

He pulled out the familiar pill bottle and tapped a small white one into his palm, then handed it back to Ollie. "Make her take this."

I eyed the pill, which now had the germs of two contaminated hands on it, and only made the briefest effort to make Ollie think I had swallowed it. I kept it tucked in my hand. He didn't say anything.

Another pill bottle came out and String dumped three yellow tablets into it and popped them into his mouth.

"There. I'm ready to drive forever," he said.

He started the Explorer and gunned the engine, jammed the gearshift lever into Drive and roared onto the highway between two eighteen-wheelers. I held my breath but we soon became part of the sparse nighttime flow of traffic.

After a few minutes my raw nerves had settled somewhat. It felt like life would never be normal again, but I had a feeling this was as close as it would come for awhile. I eyed Ollie in the corner of my vision. In a moment when he turned to stare out the window on his side I stuck the new sleeping pill into my pocket.

Eventually, the pain and horror dimmed and I sank into my seat, leaning against the door and trying to make the men believe that the sleeping pill had worked. But I couldn't get my mind off Billy, that basic, chubby guy who'd worked at a pizza place, the only one in the group who'd shown me a few small considerations. I'd never given him credit for much in the intelligence department, and I certainly never figured out his value to the gang. But he'd been decent enough. And somewhere out there was probably a family who might never know what happened to him. If I got out of this alive, I would try to find them. Try to give them some kind of comforting words by which to remember their son or brother.

I actually dozed for a short while, I think. String's voice woke me. I did the under-eyelash gaze again, scoping out the situation.

Mole slouched sullenly in the front passenger seat, giving String the occasional grunt, not exactly cooperative but I didn't sense there was a rebellion in the making either. Across the seat from me, Ollie seemed asleep. Once again, I got the feeling this was a kid who'd been shuffled around a lot and was used to doing things without question.

String, whose medication had obviously kicked in, kept up an animated chatter from the driver's seat. Road noise kept me from getting all of it, but I caught enough to figure out that we were heading for California—no surprise, considering his desperate actions to have it this way—where he thought Cristina Cross's family and/or production company would be happy to hand over the money.

Apparently, he was still set on getting five million dollars for her. Each time I thought of what would happen when he realized that he didn't have a real movie star on his hands, I got a tingling fear in my guts. The picture of Billy's bloodied body being carried out into the desert haunted me.

I tried to allay the jitters by watching for mileage signs and by trying to come up with a plan for what I would do when we stopped again. The former was a lot easier than the latter.

"You going to use that cell phone?"

The question had come from Mole, directed to String. I didn't catch the response.

"Cause you better only use it one time. Once they trace the number you better have a new phone for the next time, man."

Ollie had come awake. "Yeah, I think so too. I saw it on *CSI*. They got this map on their computers and the cell phone makes a little blinking dot, and they, like, know right where you are."

String shifted a little in his seat. "I got it taken care of. We'll get more phones."

Mole wanted to say something, I could tell, but he kept his mouth shut.

Ollie wasn't quite so savvy. "Then there was this other time on *CSI*, and they had a beacon or something right on the guy's car and they didn't even have no helicopter or nothing. They just knew right where—"

"Shut up!"

I mentally seconded that. Hadn't Ollie figured out that getting on the wrong side of this guy was not in his best interest? Privately, though, in some tiny corner of my mind I hoped that there was such a beacon on us right now. I could *really* be happy for this whole ordeal to be over.

Chapter 23

Drake spent a stomach-churning hour staying off to the side of the action. Phones rang, agents stared at computer screens and clicked away at their keyboards, but there was no breakthrough moment. Someone brought coffee. He downed two cups of it, which only added to the roiling in his stomach.

Kingston took a break and went to his own room for a shower. He emerged twenty minutes later looking amazingly refreshed. Drake ran a hand over the stubble on his own face. He should do the same. But he couldn't bring himself to leave the command room.

"Sir," one of the men at the table called out to Kingston. "This call might be of interest."

Kingston took the phone and listened intently. It was apparently a law officer from somewhere else, giving a briefing on the situation. He fired off a couple of questions about Charlie then snapped the phone shut.

"Not much news, unfortunately," he said, turning to Drake. "They've identified Leon Mohler as the man who rented two rooms with cash last night, at the same motel where the Toyota was found."

"Ch—"

Kingston shook his head. "Couldn't confirm whether there was a woman with them. The rooms were on the side of the building away from the office. The guy got busy and wasn't paying attention to what car they drove or how many people were in the group. Sheriff's men have been through the rooms but found nothing helpful. Clerk has no idea when they left. They paid cash for one night and were gone this morning."

Drake pondered that, trying to put together a scenario.

"Boss? Another call," said one of the agents.

Kingston took this one as well. He reached for a pen and jotted a few notes. "Excellent."

He turned to Drake. "A break, I hope. At least it's a strong lead. One of the vehicle reports that's come in this morning is about a 2002 Ford Explorer. It was taken from the parking lot of the same motel in Holbrook. Like I said earlier, they're starting to make mistakes."

The agent handed the page with his hasty notes to one of the men at the table. "Get this information out as an APB to all law enforcement along the I-40 corridor. This is priority. If anyone spots that Explorer they are to keep visual contact but not to approach alone. Make sure they're clear on the fact that a hostage is with these guys and that they are armed."

The other agent nodded and began rapidly entering data

into the computer.

Drake stared at the map someone had taped to the wall. If the gang headed west, the next fair-sized city they would come to would be Flagstaff. His mother lived there and Charlie might feel that was a safe place to make her move to get away. Should he call Catherine and warn her about what was going on, brief her to take Charlie in and keep her safe? He glanced at Kingston, who was still giving orders to the other officers. He could make the call privately if he used the excuse of going back to his room to clean up.

Kingston jerked and patted at a pocket. The clone of DeRon Stein's cell phone had vibrated. The agent grabbed it and looked at the readout. His face said it all. This was the call.

He let it ring three times and then hit the Talk button.

Drake was at his side in a flash, listening but only catching ragged words delivered at a fast pace.

"Slow down, I can't tell what you're saying," Kingston said, softening his voice to mimic that of the producer. He wagged a hand toward the agents on the computers, who were madly clicking away at their keyboards.

Some more fuzzy electronic voice noise.

"Why would you think that?"

Another bout of the same.

"You don't want to do that. You'll never get the money that way. The studio is insistent that I can't bring you the money without seeing Miss Cross alive and well."

Drake's gut clenched.

"Where do I bring it?" But the line went dead. Kingston stared at the dark phone.

"It'll take us another minute or two," said the agent at the table.

"I think the caller was Stringer. Mohler has a slight Spanish accent and this one didn't. Stringer is paranoid and I'd guess he's on some kind of speed right now. His voice zips along at a mile a second. He says he knows he's being followed, threatens to do away with Cristina Cross if he sees any cops."

Drake gripped Kingston's forearm. "*Any* cops? Charlie's a goner if even some traffic cop sees them?"

"You heard what I told him. Made the point that he'll never get any money if he hurts her." He pried Drake's fingers loose.

"Yeah, but—"

"He backtracked a bit then. Started talking about the money."

"But he cut you off when you asked where . . ."

"He'll call back. His reaction tells me that this is really all about the money."

The guy at the computer spoke up. "The call came from a cell phone. They're near Flagstaff."

"My mother lives there. If Charlie gets a chance to get away, she'll have a safe place to go."

"Call your mother. Give her the minimum of information but let her know that if she hears from Charlie they both need to get to a safe place. Then she needs to call us."

Kingston sent Drake a long stare.

"Under no circumstances should she have direct contact with these guys. Her life would be on the line too."

Chapter 24

A horn blared as String pulled out into traffic without looking. I gripped the edge of the seat, ready for anything. With whatever pills he'd taken, he now had the attention span of a gnat. His driving was all over the place and from what I'd gleaned of the phone call he'd just made, so were his verbal skills.

We'd pulled into the parking lot of a truck stop east of Flagstaff, where String had pulled out the new cell phone and called a number that he'd written on a small scrap of dingy paper.

He addressed the person who answered as Stein and then he rattled off a bunch of paranoid nonsense about seeing cops following us. I glanced around, hope being the eternal thing that it is, but didn't see a single sign of a lawman.

String went into a rant about killing Cristina if he so much as saw *any* cops around. Gee, that was a comforting thought. One traffic officer and I'd be toast.

The other person must have said something about that because String's next line of talk was about the money—he reiterated that it was to be five million dollars, cash—and then he told them he would call back and he ended the call abruptly. He tossed the phone into a trash barrel and off we went.

Now we were in the middle of town, the town where my mother-in-law lived, the first place we'd been, so far, where I might be reasonably sure of finding a safe haven. String passed the exit that would have led to Catherine Langston's home, then another before he decided to get off the Interstate.

"There's a Radio Shack," Mole said, pointing to a small strip-mall on the right.

String whipped into the lot, barely braking, drawing another blare of a horn from someone. I squeezed my eyes shut, hoping to survive his driving, let alone the whole ransom mess.

He parked in front of a grocery, at least two hundred yards from the wide windows fronting the electronics store. I had to give him credit for making a few smart moves along the way.

"Kid, you're coming with me," he said, turning to face Ollie. "Mole, you watch her."

Mole turned to face me, picking up the pistol that had been resting in his lap, while String tucked his own into his waistband and covered it with his shirttail. String pocketed the keys to the Explorer and I watched Ollie follow along with him toward the buildings.

My legs were achy and cramped from the hours of sitting and I gave them a little stretch. But I managed to kick the back of the driver's seat, which Mole found suspicious. He trained the gun on me and growled.

"Hey! I'm sorry you and String argued. I'm sorry that you don't have your millions of dollars yet. But don't take it out on me. I just need some exercise."

He looked momentarily taken aback by my tone. I wondered if I'd pushed a little too far, but he relaxed.

"Take 'em awhile to get those phones," he said. "We could walk around the parking lot, I guess."

"Really?" The small act of kindness was so unexpected that I nearly teared up.

"Sure." He got out first and came around to open my door, after I'd tried it myself. The SUV had those stupid backdoor locks that don't let kids escape their parents or hostages escape their captors. The pistol clearly showed through the pocket of his windbreaker, and his hand very obviously held a strong grip on it. Acts of kindness were not to become the norm, obviously.

"Stay near the car. I don't want no trouble with String, he catches you outside."

I glanced around the parking lot. Clearly, any possibility of my running away was nil. This early in the morning the lot was merely dotted with cars—no cover for me if I should dash, virtually no one around to hear a commotion. I wasn't about to test Mole's proficiency with the gun. He'd never bought into String's insistence that I be unharmed and I felt sure he wouldn't hesitate to shoot me down if I challenged him. Plus, the vision of Billy's quick demise and his body out in the desert worked wonders to keep me in line.

My legs were so stiff from inactivity that I was doing

well just to hobble around. I made a couple of small circuits, pacing off the yellow lines of a few parking spaces, tracing my way back. As my ankles and knees began to feel more flexible I did a few stretches and toe-touches. Mole stayed with me the whole time, nudging the gun against my side once or twice just to reinforce who was in charge.

"Back inside," he ordered after about five minutes.

Obviously, he didn't want me to stretch my muscles enough and get brave enough to make a run for it. Since I'd mentally been mapping out a route between cars that involved alternately running in a zig-zag pattern and dropping for cover, working my way toward the entrance of the supermarket, his concern was probably well grounded.

When I didn't move to obey, he walked up close and faced me, as if we were lovers having an intimate conversation. His breath reeked. I wondered if it would be feasible to request that someone grab us all some toothbrushes. My own mouth was none too fresh, either. I took one giant step back and walked briskly to the SUV.

At least twenty minutes went by before String and Ollie came out of the electronics store. They took their seats and minutes later we were westbound out of Flagstaff.

Tension permeated the atmosphere in the SUV. String, clearly, wasn't happy this morning. He snapped at the others whenever anyone spoke. His driving was still erratic, keeping everyone else on edge. Even Ollie, the acquiescent one, sat at his end of the back seat tense as a cat.

I chafed at the fact that we were leaving the city where I might have found safe refuge with Drake's mother. All the should-haves ran through my head. I should have bailed when we were at the side of the road in the dark last night. I should have run for it, just now, while only Mole guarded me and I was out in the open. I should be more alert to every opportunity. I know that kidnappings rarely turn out well for the victim. And in this case it would take only one misplaced word from Cristina Cross's world to let these desperate men know that they had the wrong woman.

Charlie Parker was worth nothing to them. My stomach went into somersaults every time I thought about what String's reaction would be as soon as he figured that out. My leg bounced restlessly until I forced myself to calm down. Nothing would be gained by letting them see that I was doing some heavy thinking here.

A highway sign appeared, indicating the turnoff for the Grand Canyon. String slowed. Made the turn. I had a sickening vision of the massive drop-offs, the unending miles of wilderness and millions of places where my body would never be found. I couldn't let that happen.

Mole and String controlled all the pistols. Somehow, the very next time we stopped, before we ever got to the precipice, I had to get one of the weapons. I'm a fairly decent shot at the firing range. I've experienced a couple of close encounters with people, and I've been lucky enough that I was never forced to shoot with intent to harm. But that mindset must change. I had to be ready. To save my life I needed to make up my mind that I could and would kill all three of them.

String drove the Explorer another half mile and found a spot in the middle of nowhere to pull off the road. He growled something at Mole, who turned in his seat and trained his gun straight at me. I couldn't even sneak my left hand over toward the door handle without being seen.

Meanwhile, String stepped outside. A blast of heat

whooshed in, replacing the comfy air conditioned air. Both Mole and Ollie lowered their windows to make the breeze carry through. I watched String.

He pulled out the little scrap of paper again, dialed the number. It was picked up almost immediately.

"You got the money?" he asked.

Unlike the other times he'd called, he let the other person speak for a second. They must have asked for verification that I was all right because String turned around and aimed the phone's little camera lens at me. He snapped it and started talking again.

"There. You happy? Good. This afternoon. Barstow. I'll call again with the exact time and location." He hung up before the other person could say anything more.

A hundred thoughts went through my mind but the one that rang loudest was: They're agreeing to pay?

Chapter 25

Drake got off the phone with his mother. He'd told Catherine exactly what Kingston had advised. Stay by the phone in case she should hear from Charlie. Get both of them to a safe place if Charlie should show up. He'd swallowed hard when he had to admit that his wife was in the hands of some pretty desperate men.

Catherine, bless her, didn't ask too many questions. After the initial shock she'd rallied like a trouper and said she'd be ready. She had a friend who was the former police chief. They would go to his house.

"How long before we hear back from them, do you think?" he asked Kingston.

The agent shook his head. "No idea. A few hours? Or it might not even be today."

He looked at Drake with genuine empathy. "Grab a shower if you want. Get some rest."

"I've already slept longer than I thought possible," Drake said. "But a shower would be good."

"I'll monitor your cell if you want," the agent offered.

Drake handed over his and Charlie's phones and went back to his own room. With a disposable razor, gratis from the front desk, and the tiny bottle of shampoo in his room he managed to become presentable. When he got back to the command room things had settled into a lull.

"This is the boring part," Kingston said. "Unless we get a report from law enforcement somewhere in Arizona, all we can do now is wait for their phone call."

They had pulled chairs from several of the other motel rooms, those stiff upright things that defy one to settle down comfortably. Two agents continued to monitor the computers but it didn't seem there was much to watch at the moment. Someone came in at one point with a bag of fast food breakfast sandwiches. Everyone except Drake reached for them eagerly.

An hour went by, feeling more like a day. Drake stared at the readout on his cell phone about every five minutes. No amount of willpower, it seemed, could make it send Charlie's voice over the airwaves to him. Another hour was creeping along when Kingston reacted to another vibration from the producer's phone that he kept in his pocket.

"Yeah, I've got the money," he said. "But I want to see that she's alive and well." He looked at the tiny screen on the phone and aimed a thumbs-up toward his team.

"What—" He lowered the phone. The line was dead.

"I started to ask what time," he said.

He handed the phone over to Drake. The picture was skewed and dark, but it was definitely Charlie. She had a surprised look on her face but she didn't seem to be harmed.

He studied it for a full minute before reluctantly handing it back to Kingston, who folded the phone and put it back in his pocket.

"Barstow," Kingston said. "That's where they want the money brought. Get me the logistics."

The agents on the computers tapped away furiously at their keyboards.

"There are a couple of small regional airports," Drake said. "I've flown some jobs in that area but it's been a few years ago."

"Helicopter's not going to be the quickest way to get out there," Kingston said. He chewed at his lip. "Not practical to take a whole team anyway. We'll get some of the California offices on it."

"But you're the one negotiating—"

"Right. I need to stay on this phone. Be the one to take their calls."

"I can fly you out there. We could meet up with the other teams."

Kingston debated that. A long minute went by. Then another.

Drake felt like every nerve in his body was twitching.

Kingston shook his head. "No go. Our resources are better utilized if I stay put and keep this command center set up. I can take calls from the kidnappers and then coordinate with agents on the ground in California."

He turned to one of the other agents. "Tighten the net. I want to know if that SUV is spotted. The most likely, most practical way into Barstow from Arizona is on I-40. Make it clear that the vehicle should not be approached. These guys are going to get antsy as the payoff time gets closer. Do not—repeat it when you give the order—do not let anyone stop that car."

"I could head that way," Drake said. "Surveillance by air. They won't suspect a civilian aircraft . . ."

The agent appeared to give it some thought but shook his head, nixing the idea. "I'll brief Stein on this latest development, too, and make sure he's keeping the actress and her publicist under control. Last thing we need right now is for some gung-ho paparazzi to broadcast a picture of the real Cristina Cross stepping out of a club somewhere in London."

Chapter 26

My head spun. Cristina Cross's producer or family had actually agreed to pay five million dollars? Did they not realize that she wasn't here? Why would they agree to pay to get *me* back? Surely, Drake was in touch with the authorities by now. Surely Gina at the bank had identified me as the hostage. I couldn't figure out what was going on.

And Barstow? I had no idea why String chose that location but maybe it made sense. It was no one's home turf. Neither the producer nor the gang had ties there, as far as I knew. I'd been through Barstow once, years ago. As I recalled there were several highways in and out, which would give the gang plenty of choices for their getaway. Maybe String had actually thought this through.

The upside was that, barring everything going horribly wrong, it looked like I might actually get traded for a truck full of cash and could go back home without having to shoot anyone.

String got back into the Explorer and started the engine. He had a goofy smile on his face and I couldn't tell if that was from the anticipation of a multi-million dollar payoff or if the drugs were still in his system.

"I'm hungry," he announced. He turned around and found a McDonald's in the last town we'd passed through.

As soon as I smelled that eau de French-fry coming from the exhaust fans at the place, my stomach growled in anticipation. Once again, he parked in an out of the way spot, left the engine running, and sent Ollie in for the chow. As soon as everyone had rummaged for burgers and fries we were back on Interstate 40 again.

"I don't like this," Mole said. "Being on this highway. Too open, too many cops."

I hadn't noticed a single law enforcement vehicle in ages. Trust me, I'd been watching and hoping.

"You got a map?" String challenged. "Find us another way to Barstow."

Mole pouted in his seat but String stayed with I-40. His medication must have worn off because once he'd downed the lunch he began to act sleepy. The SUV drifted toward the shoulder a time or two. Mole dozed fitfully in his seat. Ollie noticed about the same time I did, that we'd nearly edged into the side of an eighteen-wheeler.

"Hey, String, watch out!"

Ollie's shout and the deep horn of the tractor rig startled him upright again.

"Maybe we should pull over somewhere and get a little sleep," Ollie suggested.

Thank you.

String grumbled, reaching for the pills in his shirt pocket. He tipped two into his still-crimson hand and aimed them for his mouth. Ollie noticed, a moment too late, that they were the small white sleeping pills he'd been giving me, not the uppers he'd taken earlier.

"Shit, String! Now you'll be asleep for sure."

The boss didn't like the kid calling him on his mistake but at least he had the good sense to take the next exit and pull over.

"I'll drive," Mole said.

"The hell with that," String argued. "You were falling asleep too."

"What about the Kid? Let him do it."

String seemed to consider it. "Nah. I'll be fine in a few minutes."

I doubted that but wisely kept my mouth shut.

Ollie sipped at the soda he'd had with his lunch. "I gotta take a leak," he announced.

"Me too," Mole said.

Actually, I did too, but we'd stopped at the edge of an open field on the outskirts of some town that looked like it consisted of ten houses, a few eating establishments, a bank and a gas station. The midday rush hour seemed to be on; a vehicle passed us every couple of minutes, interstate drivers looking for a lunch break. There was no way I was going to squat beside the SUV here in front of half the world.

Mole and Ollie got out and stood with their backs to the car—thank goodness for small favors. String's head was already lolling against his headrest.

And that's when the solution came to me. I reached into my jeans pocket and fished out the little pills I'd hidden away. With a wary eye on String, I gently lifted the lid of

Mole's drink cup and dropped two of them in. One more went into Ollie's.

Now I just had to figure out how to keep anyone from driving this thing back into the thick of the Interstate traffic.

Chapter 27

Ican't stand this," Drake told Ron over the phone. A light breeze wafted past the shady spot where he stood. He'd walked outside the motel room and filled his brother-in-law in on the last ransom call, the possibility that Charlie was in Flagstaff, the FBI's move to start covering Barstow, California, as the probable ransom drop point. "She's out there and there's not a damn thing I can do."

"I know. I hate it too," Ron said, after relaying the information to Victoria.

Drake could hear computer keys clicking in the background.

"I've got the maps up online," Ron said. "I think Kingston's right about not heading out there with your aircraft. It's a long way, a lot of empty desert."

That information didn't help.

"Maybe I should just head back to Albuquerque. I'm

not accomplishing anything here."

"It might not feel that way, Drake. But if you weren't there we wouldn't even know as much as we do. We'd both be sitting here in the dark. Probably wouldn't hear anything at all until after they have her back."

Drake sighed. Having her back. That's all he wanted. He could pass up all the action if only that were a sure thing. But, could he skip all the drama and not know if they were getting close to finding her? Not know if she were safe, if there were a hitch with the ransom drop, if . . . He couldn't bring himself to consider the worst-case.

"I'll hold tight then, awhile longer anyway."

He hung up, with Ron's assurances that it was the best he could do. He called his mother to see if there had been any word from Charlie, although he knew there hadn't. Catherine or Charlie would have called him immediately. He stared across the highway, out toward the airport where his helicopter sat, fueled and ready to go.

"Not thinking of taking off for Barstow, are you?" Kingston's voice surprised him.

"No. Well . . . yeah. That's actually what I *was* thinking." He shoved his hands into his pockets. "But I won't do it. I thought about going back to Albuquerque. I feel useless here. But then Charlie's brother pointed out that I'd be feeling even more useless there."

"Your choice," the agent said. "Normally, a civilian— especially a family member—doesn't get anywhere near an investigation like this. But you've been helpful. I really did think that we had a shot at catching up with them at Stringer's farmhouse."

"I appreciate that. Sorry I've been jumping down everyone's throats."

Kingston shrugged. "Not that bad. I've dealt with worse."

The motel swimming pool glistened blue and silver in the sunlight. Two kids shrieked at each other, splashing and dunking, while their father loaded bags into a red car nearby. He called out to them, ordering them to get ready to leave. Life went on in such a normal way. Drake tamped down a faint resentment.

"Going to be another hot one," Kingston commented, taking a seat on a small concrete bench. "Cooler here though, with those mountains nearby, than it is in Albuquerque."

"How do you do it?" Drake asked. "Handle this like it's another day at the office, talk about the weather?"

"Sorry. I don't want you to think I'm blasé about the situation because it's not my family member." He stretched his legs out in front of him. "Believe me, I care a whole lot about resolving this case with a good outcome."

"Your retirement on the line?" Drake stopped. "Sorry. That wasn't fair. It has to be hard to retire from this kind of work, something where you're in the action all the time."

"Yeah, I guess. I got six more months. I guess the question of what I'll do next hasn't really hit me yet." He stood up. "I'm out here right now only because I've found it helpful to take a few minutes away from the intensity of the command room. It gets to you."

"Yeah. It does. I guess I'm used to putting out a fire, or taking somebody to the hospital, or rescuing someone off the side of a mountain, and then I go home and have dinner. It usually doesn't involve days and days of this . . ."

"Hours of boredom punctuated by minutes of heart-pounding terror?"

"Something like that."

The agent patted Drake's shoulder and turned to walk back toward the room.

Behind him, Drake heard a female voice. The motel manager, whom he'd seen only briefly last night, was scolding a small puppy that trailed along behind her. It was some kind of collie or setter—he wasn't sure—so small that it still had the rounded face and downy fur of a really young one. A ball of brown and white, with spots across the muzzle and chin.

"I told you, get out of here," the woman said, shoving at it with her foot. She glanced up and saw that Drake was watching her.

"Want a dog?" she asked. "Somebody dropped two of them off and I can't find a home for this one."

A hundred thoughts flashed through his head. Life was too chaotic right now to even think about adding this complication. How was he going to care for a puppy, feed it, walk it, when he couldn't even remember to eat his own meals right now? They'd both missed having a dog; recent months had felt very empty. Charlie would love it.

He stooped down and the puppy ran over to him and began licking his hands.

"It's a little girl," the woman said, obviously encouraged that he hadn't fled for the hills. "She's a sweet little thing."

The puppy climbed up the ramp of his thigh and into his arms, bringing a comforting doggy-warmth and the coffee-like scent of puppy breath.

"I'll have to take her to the shelter if I don't find a home today." That was the clincher.

He cradled the puppy and stroked her ears as he walked back toward the room where the FBI men were working.

Chapter 28

Mole nudged String, none too gently. "Trade seats with me. I'll drive awhile."

String was definitely woozy as he stepped out and walked around to the passenger side door. One down and two to go.

Mole reached for his soda and sucked down the last of it. I hadn't realized there was so little left. I held my breath for a minute but he made no comment about the taste. Ollie, after his little potty break, also drained his cup. He made a slight face at it but didn't say anything. I had no idea how quickly the pills would work, having not actually swallowed any myself, but based on the fact that String was now slumped into a dead sleep, I guessed it wouldn't be long.

I waited until Mole had started the vehicle rolling and

then tapped his shoulder.

"I need to go potty, too. But I can't do it out here in the open. Could you just cruise through town and find me a gas station or something?"

He glared at me with that why-didn't-you-say-so-earlier look that parents always give the one kid who forgot to go.

I had to stall him. We could *not* get on the Interstate with three people asleep and one, awake and terrified, sitting in the back seat. He pulled in at the first gas station we came to. It had a convenience store and that gave me an idea.

"Um . . . this is kind of embarrassing . . ." I said.

He stared at me in the rearview mirror, his eyes saying *What now?*

"Uh . . . girl stuff. Uh, that time of the . . ."

"Oh, geez. What do you want *me* to do about it?"

I glanced over at Ollie, whose eyelids were already at half-mast.

"I'll have to go inside and buy some—"

"Fine. Don't give me no details."

He shut off the engine and got out, fishing a few dollars out of his pocket. If I'd hoped that he would let me go inside alone I was soon disappointed. He walked right along with me. He wasn't quite as paranoid as String, but he wasn't taking any chances on their million dollar baby getting away.

I went to the right aisle and chose the brightest pink package they had. Mole averted his eyes as he paid and I made a show of opening the box and heading toward the women's restroom. He was yawning as I went inside.

I stalled as long as I feasibly could and then peeked outside. He'd given up standing by the restroom door and was waiting near the registers. He yawned again, hugely, but stuck right with me as I walked toward the car, my bright pink package in my hands.

"All better," I announced.

We settled into our seats and I was pleased to see that Ollie was also completely out of it now.

"Oh, look! There's an ice cream place. I'd really love an ice cream."

I have no idea why he didn't simply turn around and belt me. He had to either know that I was stalling or consider me the biggest pain in the ass in the world. When he steered toward the ice cream stand I could only attribute his compliance to the hazy feeling he must be getting from those pills.

"Hm . . . doesn't look like they have a drive-through," I said. "I'll just order at the window."

He didn't protest and he didn't leave his seat. I hopped out and walked up to the tiny order window. A teenaged girl popped her gum as she asked what I wanted. To give her a lesson in proper customer service was what I really wanted, but there was no time for that. I glanced over at Mole. His eyes were on me.

Even if I thought I had a prayer of convincing this dimwit girl to call the police without giving away the reason, I knew Mole was still being far too careful. I ordered two hot fudge sundaes.

"Here, I got you one too." I gave it my best perky voice as I handed one to him through the open window. "Looks like the other guys will miss out."

Mole seemed surprised. Maybe no woman had ever bought him ice cream before. Maybe it was just the way his eyes looked when he was struggling really hard to keep them open.

He took a spoonful of the ice cream then set the cup on the console as he backed out of his parking spot and turned toward the main drag. Darn. I'd been hoping that he would eat all of it as we sat here. It was the whole reason I ordered cups instead of cones. I spooned away at my melted fudge concoction, stopping to ask a question just often enough to gauge his level of alertness. At some point he was going to blink out in traffic and I'd have to be ready to leap over the seat and take the wheel.

He missed the entrance to the freeway—thank goodness—and then got confused about where to go. His head turned to the left and then the right as he worked to pick out a sign or landmark, something to tell him how to get back on the road to Barstow.

We were nowhere close. He'd gotten onto a narrow paved lane that didn't seem to go anywhere and by the time his head took the final dip into unconsciousness we were a couple of miles out of town. Luckily, his foot slipped off the gas pedal and the SUV began to slow to a crawl. I dropped my dirty ice cream cup into Ollie's lap and reached over Mole's shoulders and took the wheel. We cruised, ever so slowly, onto a sandy berm and the Explorer would not move another inch.

I grabbed the keys from the ignition, feeling only mildly guilty that the robbers might cook to death inside the hot car. But, hey, I was going to have to walk back to town—I wasn't leaving them with a usable vehicle.

With a wary eye on the three sleeping men, I reached into the back of the SUV, dumped all the cash from their three pillowcases into one of them and slung it over my shoulder. Then I ran for my life.

Chapter 29

The puppy licked Drake's face a couple of times and then settled into his arms, falling into that immediate limp-body sleep that puppies can do so effortlessly. He looked around but the motel manager had vanished. Unless he tracked her down and handed the puppy back, it looked like he had a new dog.

He walked into the command room to find the agents sitting around. The place had an air of delayed expectation, the lull before the event that happens when the stakes are high but there is simply nothing to do until the game starts. Two of the men glanced up at him. Smiles appeared at the sight of the little dog in Drake's arms.

"Hey, whatcha got there?" someone asked.

Kingston reached out and rubbed at the dog's ears. "Cute little guy. What kind is he?"

"She," Drake said. "I have no idea."

The group crowded around, letting the little foundling take their minds off the serious situation that had occupied them for more than three days now. They were speculating on what breed the dog might be, coming up with combinations, when Drake's cell phone rang deep in his pocket.

He handed the puppy off to someone else and yanked at the phone. He didn't recognize the number on the readout. "Drake Langston," he said.

"Honey . . . ?"

"Charlie! Oh my god, where are you? Are you safe?"

Every person in the room froze.

"I'm . . . I'm not quite sure where I am. But I'm safe." Relief flooded through him.

"I'll come get you." His voice cracked slightly, but Drake ignored the nudge from Kingston who was trying to get him to hand over the phone.

He heard her turn to someone else and ask a question.

"I stopped at a house to use the phone. The lady says we're a few miles outside Seligman, Arizona."

Drake repeated the name of the town, and the agent who'd been on the computer raced back to his seat and brought up some maps.

"Let me speak to her," Kingston insisted.

Drake gripped it tightly. "I love you, sweetheart. We'll get to you real soon." Then he handed it over to the agent, who identified himself.

"Charlie, where are your captors?" He listened to her brief answer. "Can you get to a police department, a sheriff or someone like that?" There was a long pause. "Okay, do that. Good. Yes. Probably a few hours."

Drake chafed at hearing only half of the conversation. By the time Kingston handed his phone back, he'd estimated the time it would take him to fly to her. He stepped outside the room and spoke softly, reassuring her. When he walked back inside his eyes were damp.

The agents busied themselves at the computers, giving him a minute to regain his composure.

"I can get there by helicopter in two hours," he told Kingston.

"Let's charter a plane. It'll be quicker, hold more people."

For once, Drake didn't mind someone else taking charge.

Chapter 30

The impact of the past few days began to hit me once the woman who'd let me use her phone took me to the Justice Court building in town, an unimposing one-story brown box. While she entertained a cadre of secretaries and a man who was apparently with the sheriff's department with stories of how I'd shown up at her door, a bedraggled waif, I sat in a straight-backed chair hugging a grimy pillowcase to my chest. I'd not yet told anyone what was in it.

I supposed her description wasn't too far off the mark. I couldn't remember the last time I'd brushed my hair or washed my face. I'd had only one barely-remembered shower in four days, and then dressed in the same sweaty, dirt crusted clothing with which I'd begun this whole adventure. Yeah, waif probably fit the bill.

I spotted a restroom at the far side of the room. "Mind if I . . .?"

One of the secretaries jumped up. "Oh, sure, honey. I

can't imagine what you've been through."

And I'm not supposed to tell you, I thought, remembering that FBI agent's instructions.

The woman looked a little disappointed that I didn't offer up any juicy tidbits but she ushered me toward the bathroom and pointed out where the soap and paper towels were. "Take your time, hon."

Behind the closed door, I almost collapsed. A public bathroom, reasonably clean, felt like pure luxury. I wet paper towels and used generous amounts of the smelly liquid soap—anything to wipe away both the physical and emotional dirt. My hair was hopeless. All I could was finger-comb it and hold onto the hope that I would be at home, in my own shower, very soon. I stared at the grungy pillowcase that I'd tossed into the corner.

The lumpy case was all the bank robbery had netted those guys, and now they didn't even have that. The police or FBI or whoever was involved with this would want the whole story. Thinking about the debriefing to come made me realize that I still had a long way to go before I would be home again with Drake.

When I walked back into the squad room, the deputy took over.

"We just heard from an agent Kingston," he said. His voice was soft and kind. "He says they are chartering a plane to come get you. Should be here in a couple hours."

He gave me a look of wonder, obviously guessing at how important I was to warrant a chartered flight. I didn't mention that in some people's minds I was a famous movie star. I didn't say anything at all, just nodded.

"Could we get you something to eat? Something to drink?"

A plate of Pedro's green chile chicken enchiladas and about three margaritas would be good. But again, I kept it simple. "Yes, that would be nice. Anything at all." I felt like a lot of my usual zip had somehow zipped away.

He sent someone out for a sandwich, then poured me a cup of coffee from an urn on a side table. I resumed my seat in the stiff chair, my bag of cash at my feet, and sipped the dark brew. It actually tasted amazingly good.

I resisted everyone's questions while I sat at a desk and ate my sandwich—turkey and Swiss on rye, which tasted like a banquet. Eventually the lady who'd been my ride needed to get home to her cats and the rest of them went back to their desks. I glanced at the wall clock and saw that it would still be at least ninety minutes before Drake got here, so I rested my head on my arms and fell asleep.

A small commotion infiltrated a weird dream I was having about trying to carry a bag with a million dollars in it across the desert.

Voices.

One was Drake's.

My eyes popped open and I stared around the unfamiliar room. Two men in black jeans and windbreakers, with FBI in bright yellow on the chests, were talking with the deputy who'd brought me the sandwich.

Drake was walking toward me. Nobody had ever looked so good. I tipped the chair over when I leaped up and ran to his arms. He simply held me, for a long, long time. Then there were kisses on my neck and face and I think I was kissing him back. Hysterical laughter seemed to be bouncing between us.

"I called Ron," he was saying. "And my mom. For awhile there I was hoping you would be able to get to her place."

"You knew? You knew where I was?"

"Little bits of it." He glanced toward the FBI men. "You'll need to talk to the agents. Are you up for it?"

"Do I have a choice?"

He smiled, that beautiful smile that had grabbed my heart the first day I met him. I ran my hands over his chest, wanting to feel him, to know that he was real. Wanting to hold onto him and not let go.

"I'll be with you," he said, as always divining my thoughts before I'd fully formed them.

A tall, gray-haired man with the bulk of a former football player who'd not run a hundred yards in at least thirty years introduced himself as Special Agent in Charge, Cliff Kingston. "I'm the one you talked to today, when you called your husband."

Was that only a few hours ago? The day had passed in a blur.

Kingston ushered us into an office he'd apparently commandeered, as the small facility didn't have interrogation rooms. Someone had stacked some file folders off to the side and furnished a pitcher of water and a stack of plastic cups.

The head FBI man sat behind the desk. Another one with a laptop computer positioned himself to type up my statement, while Drake and I occupied the two chairs in front of the desk.

"It's okay, Charlie. The worst is over now. Just start at the beginning."

"But what about catching them now?" I'd told someone—I thought it was the sheriff who'd been here when I first arrived—about the Explorer I'd left behind with String, Mole and Ollie in it.

"We're checking on that. For now, just tell me everything you remember."

So I did. From the moment the man with the shaky voice, who I'd later learned was Billy, grabbed me in the bank, through the whole crazy ride. He asked me to identify the two women from the place near Romeroville, but it seemed that he knew more about them than I did. All I could do was nod when he showed me their photos.

"I only saw them at a distance, from the back seat of the pickup truck," I said. "I heard two shots. I assumed the worst."

He nodded. "We found their bodies later that afternoon."

He asked me to identify other photos, mug shots of Leon Mohler and Lonnie Stringer—Mole and String. I told him the other two had been known among the gang as Kid and Domino, but in conversations with them I knew them as Ollie and Billy. He made notes about that. Apparently they'd not identified them yet.

I covered Billy's death, although I didn't have a clear idea where we were along the highway when it happened.

He told me how they'd been so close to catching up with us at Stringer Farms, and how they'd identified the place. I choked up a bit when Drake described flying in there to get me and finding me gone. He pulled my blue ponytail band out of his pocket. I ran my fingers over it as though it were some foreign object.

One of the sheriff's men tapped at the door. "We've found that Explorer you told us about. Empty."

Kingston's mouth settled in a firm line.

Drake and I exchanged a look, thinking the same thing. The three robbers were still on the loose.

Chapter 31

Drake's surprise, when we returned to Alamosa for the helicopter, delighted me. She was a wiggly bundle of brown and white warmth who leaped straight into my heart. With the mass of adorable dots across her face it was a natural that we named her Freckles.

My ordeal dimmed in a few days time and I began to settle back into my normal routine at home in Albuquerque. After that extensive debriefing and hours with a police sketch artist, the experience took on the quality of an especially vivid dream or a trip to an exotic place—indelible in my mind but somehow unreal.

The only part that nagged at me was the fact that the robbers got away. The bank had been happy at the recovery of part of the stolen loot, and even I didn't believe String or Mole would be dumb enough to return to the same city and try it again. They'd been headed for California and I hoped that's where they would stay. As for myself, I'd wanted to get back to the office immediately but both Ron and Drake insisted that I take a few days off first. I ended up spending a lot more time than I ever do in front of the television.

Media coverage of the story had, as usual, gotten a lot of the facts wrong. The robbery was reported to have netted the robbers more than fifty-thousand dollars. I'd counted two thousand in the pillowcase I brought out with me and handed over to Agent Kingston. Two of the Albuquerque stations mentioned me, identified as "a local woman who runs a private investigation firm."

Miraculously, the part about the Cristina Cross connection never got leaked to the press. I had to admire the way Kingston and his team had kept that whole bit under wraps. Once I was safe at home again, they must have let her producer know that life could proceed as usual. I saw her on some awards show in London, just a couple of days after I got home. I didn't see the strong resemblance, myself, but then I guess we never view ourselves the way others do.

Three days after my return to Albuquerque I was standing at the bathroom mirror, realizing that my hair seriously needed trimming.

"Hey you," Drake said from the doorway. "Brought you some coffee."

It's amazing how solicitous a guy will get when you've been away for a few days.

"Thanks." I took the mug and enjoyed a long sip.

"You sure you're okay with me taking that photo shoot?" he asked.

"Absolutely. I'm just glad they still wanted to do it after you had to cancel the original date."

"Me too. But I'll be glad to cancel again if you're uneasy about being home alone."

I tossed a wet washcloth at him.

This is the other thing about surviving a dangerous situation. We'd been out to the gun range twice in the past three days, he bought me pepper sprays enough for all my jacket and jeans pockets, and he'd already begun encouraging Freckles into a frenzy whenever anyone came to the door. All the attention was beginning to wear—just a little—and I really could use an evening to kick back with a good book.

I dabbed on some lipstick and rubbed my lips together, then bent down and called to the puppy. "Hey, Freckles! C'mere baby."

She scrambled into the room, four paws slipping and going all directions on the tile floor. We still haven't figured out what breed she is—probably a mixture—so the whimsical name has just stuck. I jostled the little ball of fluff and kissed her on the nose. It's amazing how well she has filled the empty spaces in our lives where a dog really belongs.

"Okay, then," Drake said. "As long as you have 'killer' here to guard you . . ."

I scooped up the fuzzy brown and white bundle and carried her along as I followed Drake to the front door, kissed him and wished him luck with the job.

Ten minutes later I was on the way to the office, puppy at my side, to face the mountain of mail and calls that were probably awaiting me. I pulled around to the back of the gray Victorian, the Jeep finding its familiar parking spot beside Ron's Mustang and Sally's minivan, one more detail on the pathway back to normal life.

Freckles immediately raced around the yard, finding all

the scents of her predecessor and any strange wild critters that might have wandered in recently. I gave her a couple of minutes but finally had to insist that we get to work. She zoomed toward the back door at my call, all flapping ears and scurrying paws. My heart did a little flip and I laughed at her antics.

Inside, the kitchen was deserted. Even the coffee carafe, which is normally ready by now, was gone. Ron must have carried it to his own office upstairs. Sally was no doubt at her reception desk, probably eager to catch me up on office happenings. I'd already talked to her on the phone and told her what I could about my own adventure.

I let the puppy sniff around the kitchen while I meandered toward Sally's desk. The whole place seemed a little too quiet.

Two seconds later, I knew why, when a dozen people in the reception area shouted "Surprise!" It was a good thing I hadn't followed Drake's advice and walked around with my gun drawn. I could see a light fixture or two meeting their demise.

Familiar, smiling faces watched my utter shock.

"Welcome home, Charlie." Sally rushed forward to hug me.

Victoria and Ron stood near the stairs, he grinning like the sneaky brother that he is. When my heart stopped pounding like a drum, I looked around and took stock. I spotted my good friend Linda Casper, and there was Gina from the bank. She rushed toward me with tears in her eyes.

"Oh, Charlie, I'm so, so sorry that this happened to you."

I tried to reassure her that I really was just fine. She'd

probably been more terrified than I, at the moment those guys hauled me out the door.

A few clients were here and I did my best to play up Ron's involvement in tracking the bad guys and getting me back. No harm in putting our little investigation business in the best possible light.

Kent Taylor, the APD homicide detective with whom I've had a few encounters—mostly friendly—stood near Ron. I noticed he was eyeing a cake that sat on the conference table, right by the missing coffee carafe.

Sally bustled forward and tapped on the table to get everyone's attention. This sent the puppy into a frenzy and it took a minute to reassure her that there was no intruder-crisis.

Sally gave a little welcome-home speech that started me dabbing at my eyes, especially when she said that the cake had come from my favorite bakery in Taos and that she'd driven up there to Sweet's Sweets to pick it up yesterday afternoon. Well, that was the clincher—a fabulous cake, and a lot of effort to get it. By the time she finished talking everyone in the room was looking around for tissues.

I performed the honors of cutting my cake—a triple chocolate torte, filled with raspberries and trimmed in shaved almonds. I'm afraid that anyone who spoke to me in the next ten minutes got a mumbled, crumb-filled answer. There was no way I was skipping my share of that fabulous confection.

The crowd dispersed soon after, to duties in their own workplaces. I carried the remains of the cake to the kitchen and stowed it in the purple bakery box. Ron and Kent Taylor were standing there.

"Glad you're all right," Taylor said. He reached out and

gave me a pat on the arm, probably the most caring gesture he'd ever shown toward me. "You had a lot of us pretty worried."

Awww . . . How sweet.

But Ron's face looked serious. "Is there anything new about the suspects?" he asked.

Taylor shook his head. "It's not part of my division, but I don't think so. I talked with Dave Gonzales yesterday and he thinks they probably headed for California. One of the men had ties there, I guess."

I remembered something said during one of the endless days in the car, but when I'd mentioned it to the FBI men during my interview it didn't seem like enough to really put them on the trail of the robbers.

Taylor was giving me the eyeball. "Don't you go getting involved in finding them, Charlie. There are plenty of law enforcement folks on this case already."

Professionals, he meant. Well, fine with me. I'd seen all I ever wanted to see of those guys. I caught Ron staring at the cake box so I picked it up and carried it to my office. He could have more, but no way was he sneaking the whole thing while I wasn't watching.

Freckles followed me up the stairs, her short legs barely clearing the risers. I had a feeling that situation wouldn't last for long. In just these few days she'd already grown and I wouldn't be surprised if we were dealing with a good-sized dog before long.

She raced ahead, poking into each of the offices and the bathroom, almost immediately finding the tin of dog biscuits I'd always kept on my bookshelf. She plopped her little bottom to the floor and stared up at it wistfully. Well, what can I say? It was so darn cute that I had to give her one. Who's training whom here, anyway?

Watching the dog was, I must admit, just an excuse not to look at my desk. Sally had done her best to sort it and get rid of the junk that she knew I would have tossed out anyway. She'd handled some correspondence and left copies of the letters for me to read and file away. My accounting duties were mostly what remained and I settled happily into the realm of receivables, payables, and payroll taxes. Weird, I know.

Somewhere around noon, Ron stuck his head around the doorjamb and asked if I'd like to go out for some lunch. Since this almost never happens I should have jumped at the chance but I felt like I was just hitting my stride. There were a zillion computer entries to make and I didn't especially want a break—plus I had already sneaked a second piece of cake.

"When I get back, maybe we can go over a couple of new cases," he suggested.

I nodded, without taking my eyes off my computer screen.

"Want me to bring you a sandwich?"

Another nod. "Anything light." That was like telling Emeril to leave out the butter. Ron gave me a puzzled look and left.

Another hour must have passed. Somewhere in there he came back and put a ham sandwich on my desk. Sally buzzed me on the intercom to let me know that she was leaving for the day. She still likes her half-day schedule, picking up her little girl from kindergarten and being home to spend time with her hubby. Can't blame her for that.

The bars of sun coming through my bay window completely changed angle, the next time I noticed. I'd gotten out of my chair twice to take the puppy outside but otherwise, it came as a surprise to me that it was nearly six o'clock when Ron stepped into my doorway.

"Never did get to those new cases," he said. "And now I have to run. Promised Victoria a date night."

I nodded. She and I had never made up our missed lunch from last week. I supposed I should suggest some kind of girls-day-out. It's just that I'm not real big on that stuff. The whole mani-pedi-spa thing always seemed like it would eat into my time for balancing ledgers, flying helicopters or chasing down bad guys.

I waved him out the door with a promise that we'd talk about the cases tomorrow.

At some point I noticed that the puppy was getting restless. Poor little thing was learning the hard way what a workaholic mom she had.

"Okay, we'll go home." I shut down the computer and tamped some invoices into a stack for tomorrow. Gathering my purse and the dog's leash, I switched out the lights and we headed downstairs. Sally had set the answering machine and Ron left the night lamps on. All I had to do was coordinate getting the back door locked while dealing with a hyped-up puppy on a leash.

I ended up deciding to get the dog to the car first and then go back to lock up. The leash and purse went into the back seat and then I gave short-stuff a boost to the passenger seat in front. I'd just double-checked the lock on the kitchen door when I sensed movement behind me. The hair on my neck rose.

"Hello, Charlie." The voice was String's.

Chapter 32

String stepped from behind the lilac bush at the corner of the building, pointing that very familiar pistol at me.

No way. Before I could give it a second thought I grabbed a pepper spray canister from my jeans and shot him full in the face with it. He dropped the pistol, screaming and grabbing at his eyes.

I ran for my Jeep, dove in and fumbled through my keys with shaking hands. I snapped the electric door locks. The dog went into a frenzy, zipping around inside the car and barking like crazy as I started the engine and threw the thing in gear. I roared around the side of the office, only to find a strange vehicle in the driveway, blocking me.

Someone sat in the front passenger seat.

Mole.

Without a second thought I whipped the wheel to the

left, taking out a flower bed and leaving tracks across the lawn. It felt like I flew off the curb and then I hit the street with a hard jounce.

One backward glance showed that Mole was getting out of the other car. I didn't stick around long enough to find out any more than that.

How had they found me? Questions raced through my head about as fast as my Jeep was racing through the streets. I made several quick turns through our quiet residential area, cut over to Central and turned west. Then it hit me.

If they'd found my office, they might very well know where I lived.

I couldn't go home.

I kept going straight, heading across the river. At Coors Road I turned north. This part of town has grown so quickly in recent years that I couldn't be sure what I would find, but at least there were lots of choices. I spotted a crowded, well-lit shopping center and pulled in. Parked in a spot surrounded by other cars, facing outward for a quick getaway.

My hands shook as I plucked my cell phone from my purse. Poor little Freckles was shaking beside me on the seat. What an introduction to life with Charlie. I pulled her onto my lap and petted her while I tried to think about what to do next.

I didn't want to deliver this news to Drake yet, knowing he might still be in the air. I called Ron instead.

"I don't think I better go home," I said, after explaining the melee at the office.

"No. I wouldn't chance it."

"I've got the number of that Agent Kingston," I said. "Somewhere here . . ." I rummaged one-handed through my purse, holding the phone with the other.

"Good. Call him. See what he advises. Do you want us to come out there?"

I pictured Victoria being very unhappy at the idea of his leaving their date night to come rescue the perpetually troubled little sister.

"No, I don't see any need for that. I'll figure out where to go and then I'll call you."

I clicked off the call and punched in Kingston's number. He answered on the second ring. It was probably pretty rare that an FBI agent gave someone his personal cell number, so he must have known it was important.

"I was afraid of that," he said, after I explained. "Hoping that those guys would stay in California was probably too wishful."

"So, what should I do?"

"Is there a friend or neighbor you could stay with?"

I thought through my list. The neighbor who would take me in without a second thought (because she's already done so several times) is my surrogate grandmother, Elsa Higgins. But her house is right next door to mine. Going there wouldn't keep either of us very safe.

Paranoia kicked in. I couldn't shake the idea that if String had found out my real identity and where I worked, he could track all my friends as well.

Kingston must have read my mind. Or maybe I said some of this out loud. "Look, he can't know everything and he can't be everywhere. I'm getting some agents out to watch your house and your office. They'll be there within the hour. You should be safe enough with them around."

I hung up, every shred of skepticism working its way to the surface. Hey, I watch a lot of movies, and when the lone woman is told that the police are right outside, guarding her, something always happens. Always.

I pictured String and Mole—royally pissed because I'd taken their money and left them with groggy hangovers from the sleeping pills. I had no illusions about getting away as easily a second time.

A cluster of motels and truck stops surrounded the area near the I-40 onramps. I passed them all up and drove several miles north where another bunch of hotels catered to the business traveler and the huge west-side Intel plant. Parking my Jeep in the lot of one such place, I walked about half a mile and checked into another one.

The desk clerk gave me an odd look. Obviously frazzled woman clutching a puppy under her arm and a cell phone in one hand, while struggling to keep a purse strap over the shoulder . . . the guy couldn't figure out what my story was. But at least he didn't ask. He took my credit card and handed me a plastic key.

I settled into a plain vanilla room and bolted the door every way I could. Freckles dashed about, checking out her third set of new surroundings in nearly as many days. Life must be quite the adventure to her.

For my part, I was getting a little sick of the adventure and just wanted to move about freely in my own hometown without fear that some bad guy lurked in the bushes. I took stock of the room with its faux-Euro bedding and flat screen TV, noticed it had a mini bar and used it to make myself a fairly stiff rum and Coke.

Once the drink coursed its little version of relaxation therapy through me, I thought I finally had it together well enough to call Drake. I made light of the situation, saying that I'd spotted two of the bank robbers near the office and just felt it better to be away from my familiar haunts tonight.

He was tired, I could tell. The past week had been sheer hell for him and now he was feeling the pressure of keeping the helicopter busy on some paying jobs. Gotta make those outrageous insurance payments. I gave him the name of the hotel and my room number.

"I'll meet you at the airport when you fly in tomorrow, if you'd like," I said.

"Maybe I should join you in that hotel." By the tone of his voice I knew he wasn't *that* tired.

"Umm . . .good idea." Although I really couldn't see how a romantic interlude was going to happen, talking about the possibility definitely lightened my mood as I hung up.

Unfortunately, the romance bubble popped a moment later when my cell phone rang. Ron.

"Where are you?" he asked with more than a hint of grumpiness in his voice. "You were going to call Kingston and then call me right back."

"Sorry." I filled him, letting him know that I didn't completely trust the FBI or the Albuquerque police to keep wily guys like String and Mole away from my house or office.

"I'm in a hotel now, but I'm a little worried about Elsa. If those guys know where I live and they're hanging around waiting for me to go home, and if she sees them and questions what they're doing there . . ." I could just picture my eighty-something neighbor demanding answers from a guy like String.

"I'll go by and check on her. Meanwhile, give her a call and tell her not to open the door to anyone."

Trying to warn her about the danger and that she might

spot cop cars around the house without really telling her why was no easy sell. Elsa still thinks of me as that teenager she took into her home after my parents died, and she doesn't really take "don't worry about it" as an answer. I did my best and told her to expect Ron within a few minutes. Let him cover the tough questions.

Gradually, the toll of the long day and the scare began to coalesce into a dull fatigue in my bones. I took a shower and turned on the television, relying on old reruns of *Frasier* to lift my mood and take my mind off real life.

Freckles curled up next to me and her warm little body worked to reassure me that there really are good things in this world. Somehow, I slept in a deep, dreamless state until I began to hear the morning movements of other guests opening and closing their doors along the corridor.

I stretched and hugged the puppy before it hit me that the new day was beginning with a big question: Now what?

Chapter 33

I threw my clothes back on, walked Freckles outside, grabbed a bagel and cup of coffee from the free breakfast bar provided by the hotel, and decided I better take stock of the day. I couldn't live like this, in a hotel room, wearing the same clothes day after day, trying to care for a puppy and not even being able to go to my home or office in my own hometown. It was ridiculous.

A call to Kingston netted me the answer that they were still watching my place but had seen no trace of the bad guys. I expressed my frustration.

"I'll get you an escort," he said. "Someone to go with you wherever you need to go."

Gee, that wasn't going to be a whole lot better than having the 24/7 company of the gang, now was it? At least this time the guns would be pointed away from me instead of toward me. I grumbled, but agreed.

"Can I make contact with the agents watching my house? I need to get some things, food for the dog, stuff like that."

"I was about to send the overnight watch crew home. I'll meet you there myself."

Whatever.

"Twenty minutes?" That was wishful, I knew, in the morning rush traffic, but I couldn't sit around here much longer.

He said he'd be there.

Forty-five minutes ticked by and I fumed the whole time, unaccustomed as I'd become to driving across this city during the heaviest traffic hours. But eventually I pulled into my driveway, feeling on hyper-alert for anything unusual. Everything seemed just fine, including the dark agency car out front. Kingston stepped out of it as I exited the Jeep.

"I walked around back, checked all the windows and doors. Everything looks good," he said.

"Maybe they aren't as bright as we're giving them credit for," I said with a wistful little tone in my voice.

"Don't get too complacent. The fact that they came back to Albuquerque tells me they're pretty desperate. Your name wasn't mentioned on the news, so we can't discount that they had some way to figure out who you were and where your office is."

My guts tightened up again. Just when I'd begun feeling a tiny bit less vulnerable.

I stared at my front door.

"Charlie, I'd recommend that you stay hidden away for a few more days. Give us the chance to use our resources and catch these guys."

It probably made sense but the instructions chafed at

me. "Give me fifteen minutes," I told him.

Freckles followed me onto the porch and I unlocked the front door. She dashed past me, into the living room. A small sheet of paper drifted across the hardwood floor at the entry. I bent to pick it up but stopped cold.

"Agent Kingston," I called out. "You better come see this."

Bold words in black marker covered the page: *You took our money.*

Kingston appeared at the open front door. I pointed at the note.

"They must have slipped it under the door," I said. "When could they have done that?"

"Sometime before my agents arrived. They watched the place all night and no one approached this door."

I went back over the previous afternoon in my head. It was nearly dark when I left the office and encountered String. After I made my mad dash across the lawn and over the curb they must have come here and left me this warning. They may have even staked out the house, hoping I would come right home, until the government cars began showing up in the neighborhood.

Kingston picked up the note by one corner and went out to his vehicle to get an evidence bag for it.

"Not that we need more proof about where this came from," he said, "but every little bit helps make the case in court."

Yeah, I supposed that once I was dead it would be helpful to prove who'd come after me.

"I hope I don't have to argue with you about being extra careful," the agent said.

I put a hand on my fluttering stomach. "No. No

argument here."

"I'll wait with you until you pack a few overnight items. You should go back to the hotel." He stepped inside and closed the front door. I watched him go to the front window and take a position so that he faced my Jeep in the driveway, peering through the sheer drapes.

While he stood vigil, I gathered all the new amenities we'd purchased for Freckles—crate, blankets, food, dishes, leash and toys. It's amazing how much stuff a new baby needs. Then I packed a small bag for myself.

"I want to check with my elderly neighbor," I told Kingston. "It will just take a minute."

Without waiting for an okay, I dialed Elsa's number.

"I'm making a vacation out of it," she said, after telling me she'd talked to Ron last night. "My cousin in Portland is always begging me to visit. This looks like a good time. Your brother is picking me up at noon and taking me to the airport."

Bless her. What a trouper she is.

I felt about a million percent better when I hung up. I called Ron's cell immediately and told him to watch her until she was safely past security in the airport. He acted as if I were treating him like an idiot for telling him all this. Maybe I was. Everything felt extremely jumbled up right now.

My small suitcase joined the stack of doggie goodies by the front door.

"Are there any leads at all?" I asked Kingston. "Anything on these guys' whereabouts?"

"We questioned all known relatives of Stringer and Mohler, right after we got you back from Arizona. As of last night we've had someone watching each of their homes. Put the word out among informants on the street."

"And . . . nothing?"

"It can take time. Guy like Mohler, with his history of drug deals, he's gonna show up at his old haunts eventually."

Eventually. That sounded like a long time to me.

"Ready?" he asked. He walked out to the porch ahead of me, scanning the street carefully. I had to give the guy points for trying to keep me safe.

I put the loaded dog crate and my own bag in the back of the Jeep and coaxed Freckles up to the passenger seat.

"I'll be at my office," I told him.

"That's not—"

"It's happening. It may not be the safest place, but I have a job to do and I've already been away from it too long. I'll go to a hotel tonight."

"Before nightfall. And don't walk outside alone, not out the door, not down the street." He stood beside my door, his eyes scanning the street as we talked.

Sheesh. I gritted my teeth. Taking orders goes against my grain and hiding out is definitely not my lifestyle.

"At the office, keep all the doors locked. Instruct your people to admit only known persons." He caught my erupting protest. "I wouldn't put it past these guys to try to force their way in."

"Surely they don't think I have their money?"

He held up the plastic bag with the note. "Well, you *are* the one they're coming to. They seem to think you can get that bank money back for them."

Valid point. But so illogical. I fumed as I locked my doors and started the Jeep. Kingston went back to his vehicle and I could see him talking on a handheld radio.

I spotted two strange vehicles on the street where our

office is, a van with the windows darkened—way too shiny and new for String or Mole. The little antennae spiking up from its roof spelled 'government.' Same for the gray car with two guys in suits, about half a block away. I gave them a tiny wave as I passed.

Both Ron's and Sally's vehicles were parked in their usual places. An armed man in uniform stepped out from behind the ancient elm tree at the corner of the property when I pulled in. Once he saw it was me, he blended back into the shrubbery. I sighed.

Ron had apparently gotten the new office protocol too. The back door was locked and the pull-down shades were closed. I unlocked my way in and called out. No telling how edgy everyone else might be by now.

At least the coffee machine was full. I retrieved the bakery box with the remains of yesterday's decadent chocolate cake from my office and it didn't take more than a couple of minutes for both Sally and Ron to show up.

"So." I didn't know what else to say.

"So. So, I guess we wait this out," Ron said.

I looked over at Sally. "You don't have to be here."

Ron piped up. "We've already discussed it."

"I'll stay until my normal time today," Sally said. "That way, someone is with you until Ron gets back from the airport."

"Depending on how things go," I told her, "I'd rather that you stay home tomorrow and until these guys are caught. Even though they didn't harm me before, there's no telling what they might do now."

She nodded. I also noticed that she gulped.

"You've got a small child, a husband who needs you. I don't want to put you at risk."

"I know. We were already talking about going away for the weekend. I'll convince Ross that we should do it."

"Good."

She gave me a long hug. "I'd stay if it would help you out."

"I know you would. But it's not necessary." I turned and rummaged through a drawer for a knife to cut the cake.

Ron sent a worried look at me, behind Sally's back. He said, "Okay, that's the plan. I'll be back from the airport before one o'clock and then you'll join up with your family and take a nice little summer vacation."

"With pay," I added, handing her a plate with a thick slice on it.

She headed back to her desk and I turned to Ron.

"Okay. That plan gets us through to early afternoon. What then?"

The quick answer came when my cell phone rang, down inside my pocket. Drake.

"Hi, hon. Everything going all right this morning?" Rotor noise filled the background.

"So far, so good," I said, raising my voice a bit. "How about you? Job done?"

There was an affirmative answer but the background noise was getting louder.

"Do you still want me to pick you up when you get here?"

"Well, that's the thing. I got a call. There's a brush fire south of Los Lunas and I need to go there. Will you be all right?"

Poor guy. He'd taken so much time off this past week to watch out for me. I couldn't ask him to pass up any new jobs.

I assured him that I'd be fine but told him about Kingston's instructions to stay in a hotel again. We agreed to touch base later in the day.

Ron had disappeared with a hunk of cake and I found him in his office.

"Okay, what next?" I said, leaning against the doorjamb. "I hate living on the run from these guys. And you know good and well that the minute the FBI gets a more urgent call this case will go straight to the back burner."

He nodded, which sent chocolate crumbs all over his shirt front.

"I can't keep living in hotels, watching every shadow on the windows."

"Kingston says they are watching for Stringer and Mohler around their old haunts. But that won't last long."

"Exactly. It's fine to think that I have some protection out there, Ron, but I'm not good at waiting around. I have to be proactive."

I walked over to his window that faced the street. Both the van and the car were still in place. For now.

"You have your weapon with you?" he asked.

I patted my purse.

"Keep it on your person. You leave the purse in your desk when you go downstairs. You should have it where you can get your hands on it."

I wanted to resent the advice, but had to admit that the gun—in my purse, in the car—had done me no good yesterday. It was having the pepper spray in my pocket that saved my bacon that time. I set the purse on his desk, retrieved the pistol and stuck it into my waistband. It was heavy, uncomfortable, and reassuring.

"I have a ton of invoicing to do," I said. "Pop over across the hall if you come up with a plan for what we should do next."

I settled at my desk and Freckles lay at my feet. The bonding was pretty cute to watch. Better than watching for bad guys any day.

Emails, invoicing, and computer entries soaked up my attention for awhile. Longer than I imagined, because the next thing I knew Ron was standing there. In his hand, a sheet of paper.

"Found these addresses," he said. "Last known residences of Stringer and Mohler, plus some for relatives. I think I'll do a little drive-by of my own, now and then. The third guy—can't find anything without a last name."

"I never knew what it was. The older men called him Kid. Billy, the younger one who was killed, called him Ollie. That's not a lot to go on."

"I think I'll put in a call to Detective Gonzales. Based on what their sketch artist did when you worked with him— maybe they've come up with something. I don't know how much Gonzales will tell me, but we'll see."

I'd given it a lot of thought in recent days but still didn't really have any firm information I could offer about the third man. He seemed so innocent—well, maybe naïve was a better word—in retrospect. The teenager who'd somehow gotten in with a couple of really bad dudes. Considering what had happened to Billy, I wondered if Ollie were even alive now.

Chapter 34

Oliver Wendell Trask crouched beside a blue dumpster in a dark, stinking alley. His hands were coated in grime. His hair and clothing reeked of used cooking grease and rotted vegetables from a quick foray into the dumpster for anything edible.

Mama would have belted him across the mouth for consuming the stuff he'd just put in there, a half-eaten burger and a few ribs with some of the meat still on them. But that was back when she still cared what he ate, when she cared whether he bathed. By the time he'd hit high school the daily battles became too much for either of them. She'd run off with some guy, one of the many. He'd dumped the pretense of attending classes and fended for himself ever since.

He looked at his hands and cringed. He wasn't fending all that well right now, for sure. This whole week had turned into a pile of crap.

A door opened and a man in white kitchen garb stepped out and flung two bulging bags into the open trash bin. Ollie pressed himself into the wall at his back but the man saw him anyway.

"What're you doing here? Get moving!"

Ollie leaped to his feet and ran down the alley. There just wasn't enough fight left in him for another confrontation. Not like there used to be, even a few days ago. The day he'd questioned String about his share of the bank money. That turned into a nasty scene with String taking aim at Ollie with that pistol. Ollie scrambling to get away, bumping into String, making him shoot a hole in the ceiling of some trailer they'd broken into and spent their first night back in Albuquerque. He'd been on the run ever since.

He reached the mouth of the alley and stared at the street. Didn't recognize this part of town. Didn't really matter. He had no money, no car, no place to go. He waited for a clear spot in the traffic and dashed across to a small park. Streetlights cast small puddles of golden light around the edges of it, but the middle was a black mass of bushes and trees. He headed for the darkest area and flopped to the ground with his back against the trunk of some huge tree.

The whole dream had turned out so badly. His plan—the house for Rena Lynn, the convertible, their life together—it seemed so far away now. He'd tried to call her, two days ago when he still had a few coins in his pockets. An answering machine came on—when had they gotten that?—and the pay phone wouldn't give him back his money. He thought of trying to call Sadie, but wasn't at all sure that his mother would accept a collect call from him. And that would depend on locating her anyway. They hadn't spoken in three years and it wouldn't surprise him if she'd found herself a new man by now. She might not even live in this city anymore.

No, he wasn't that desperate yet.

He'd passed a twenty-four-hour Laundromat earlier in the day. This late, there might be a good chance of finding it empty. He could wash up in the restroom. Might even find some clean clothes. Could probably figure a way to get some money out of the place. Those little cash businesses—a place like that would be full of dollar bills and coins and everything.

He would clean up, find enough money for real food, and then he'd call Rena Lynn again. Or maybe he'd ride the bus up to her place. They could still run off together, even without the money he'd hoped for. Her dad gave her a car when she graduated last month, a used Honda. Pretty nice little ride, even if it wasn't exactly a hot car. It would get them out of Albuquerque and then they could find a place to get married and settle down. To hell with String and his big plans.

Chapter 35

Ron had called in sometime around mid-afternoon. Besides cruising past the addresses he'd gotten for relatives of String and Mole, we did still have a business to run here. He'd gone down to the courthouse to research some records for one of the law firms that regularly hires us.

Paperwork finished by five o'clock, I was really in the mood to go home for a long nap on the couch, followed by making a nice dinner for Drake. But with my husband out fighting a fire—we never knew how long those could go on—and me living in a hotel with neither comfy couch nor my own kitchen facility, probably the best I could hope for was a night of TV in a generic room.

Freckles had snoozed the afternoon away beside my desk, in almost the exact spot her predecessor always chose, but now she was up and restless. And a restless puppy should never be ignored. We weren't all that certain of her house training just yet. She raced me down the stairs and to the back door, but I wasn't keen on dashing out there to find another surprise visit from an unwelcome guest.

I clipped the leash onto her tiny collar and led her to the front door instead. A peek out the side glass reassured me that the FBI van was still in place, two doors down. I scanned the street. The man behind the wheel of the gray car raised his fingers in salute and I gave a tiny wave back. All looked normal.

Finished with her business, Freckles pulled me back to the front door. She was gaining strength every day and I had a feeling leash training better be in the plan pretty soon. At our initial visit to the vet, the day after we'd brought her home, the doctor said we could expect her to grow up to fifty pounds or so. I needed to establish early on just who was really in charge here. In keeping with that, I followed her into the kitchen and filled her food bowl.

While she wolfed through her food I phoned the agents out front to let them know I was ready to leave, then put away my files, shut down the computer and turned out the lights upstairs. Rechecked the front door and windows, turned on the proper night lights and worked my way to the back door and peeked out the window. The uniformed officer stood near my Jeep, which was reassuring. If only it always worked this smoothly.

But when I opened the back door to leave, a piece of paper fluttered to the kitchen floor. The bold black marker strokes were way too familiar.

You owe me $50,000.

Chapter 36

The plan went pretty smoothly. Ollie found the Laundromat, even though it was a bit farther than he'd remembered. Bright fluorescent lighting cast white squares across the sidewalk out front and from a vantage point at the dark side of the parking lot he could tell it was empty. He walked in, hoping the air conditioning would offset the heavy summer night but a couple of dryers were running, gobbling up any coolness from the big overhead register. He checked some doors at the back of the place. One went into an empty bathroom, the other was locked—probably a supply closet or something. At least there was no one around.

He rummaged through the dryers and came up with a pair of jeans and T-shirt that would fit him. He closed the dryer door and tossed the clothing into the restroom, in case their owner showed up.

With a casual swagger, he cruised past the change machine, a thing that would fill your hands with quarters if you just fed in enough dollar or five-dollar bills. The boxlike metal had been welded repeatedly and looked stronger than Fort Knox.

An industrial sized padlock held it all together. He gave a tug. It was tight enough to protect an armored car. Well, shit.

Ollie helped himself to a washcloth from the bounty in the dryer and went into the restroom where he did a respectable wash-up—what his mother would have called a spit-bath—and changed into the clean clothes. He heard a sound and peeped out through a crack near the doorjamb.

A set of headlights pulled up to the front of the place and a harried looking woman in a waitress uniform jumped out of a small white car. She rushed in, opened the dryer door and patted the clothes inside. They were dry enough to suit her and she heaped them into the basket she'd brought with her, then bustled back out to the car and was gone within minutes.

Okay, the danger of being caught in someone else's clothes was gone. But he still had no cash. He eyed the door next to the bathroom. Locked doors always intrigued him. They didn't usually stop him either. With a glance back at the front windows to be sure no one was watching, he backed up and gave a hard kick. The deadbolt lock held tight, but the hollow-core door splintered. Two more kicks and he got his hand inside. A twist of the deadbolt and he was in.

Cartons of those tiny soap boxes lined one wall. A mountain of paper towels and toilet paper rolls filled another corner. In the middle of the room stood an industrial sized mop and bucket, and some brooms leaned against the shelving that held the paper towels. As his father would have said, all that stuff was as useless as tits on a boar.

But maybe . . . He spotted a metal toolbox on the floor. No rings of keys to unlock the trove of coins in the machines—dammit—but a quick search did net him a hefty pry bar.

"That's better," he muttered.

Back at the change machine he debated how to tackle the heavy padlock. The pry bar didn't have much effect when he tried to snap it open. But one of the welds on the strapping that held the machine to the wall looked a little weak. He applied all the torque he could muster.

He felt something move. A little more pressure. A little more shift.

Something about the sound of the air conditioning changed, a subtle altering of the air in the building. He turned around.

"Freeze right there!"

A damn cop, holding a gun on him.

"You're under arrest."

He dropped the pry bar and watched his whole plan vanish into thin air.

Chapter 37

I must have shrieked, just a tiny bit, when the sheet of paper fluttered to my feet, because the officer out by my car came running toward me.

"How did this get here?" I demanded.

He stammered a little while I built up more steam.

"Weren't you here all afternoon? How did someone get up to this door? How did they plant this note?" I eyed the back fence, which divided our property from a similar one on the street to the north.

He reached for his shoulder-mike and mumbled some kind of numerical code, not even attempting to answer my questions. In about five seconds two more men came running up the driveway, the guys from the gray car. Good. I'd like to hear how he explained this to them.

We spent another ten minutes with a whole lot of

mumbo about did I recognize the handwriting, did I think it was from the same sender as the last one, and a bunch of other questions that could be answered with "well, *yeah*—." Someone finally called Agent Kingston and he made the sensible suggestions that they bag the note and that someone should escort me to my hotel and see that I was in for the night safely.

And somehow, even though that hadn't sounded so appealing an hour ago, it was looking pretty good now. I'd chosen a different hotel and made a reservation earlier in the day, opting for one that was somewhat closer than the far northern end of Coors Road and which would put me on the tenth floor in a class of hotel where anyone the likes of String or Mole would stand out and immediately be spotted by onsite security. This business of avoiding kidnappers sure could get expensive.

I checked in with Drake and told him my new location. He was fifty miles from home and the fire boss wanted him to stay at the hasty base camp they'd set up, to assure that he would be available again at daybreak. Looked like it was room service for Freckles and me.

Sick of fast food and cheap motels—or maybe it was simply that my recent experiences of sleeping on couches and floors was still too fresh—I splurged on a meal and wine that set me back almost as much as the cost of the room where I'd stayed last night. Call me a snob but I felt like it was about time to treat myself a little better.

I set Freckles' little crate under a painting that purported to be an RC Gorman, closed the floor-to-ceiling drapes, and nestled into my 500-count sheets, with a comforter that must have been stuffed with dandelion fluff on top of me. And thus I stayed, without rolling over once, until my cell phone rang on the nightstand.

The bedside clock said it was 5:12 a.m.

"Ms. Parker? This is Detective Dave Gonzales, APD."

I think I groaned. Would there ever again be a time in my life that I could go a whole day and night without at least one call from law enforcement?

"We're holding a suspect downtown that we think might be the third man from the bank robbery. I know this is a lot to ask, but could you come down and identify him?"

I sat up in bed and scrubbed sleep grains out of my eyes. "Now?"

"He's going over to a cell in the Detention Center in about an hour. After that, it gets a little harder to arrange all this. If you could take a look while we still have him in an interrogation room it really simplifies things."

"It will take me a little while to get organized." I was surprised I could even think about being organized this early. Must have been because I fell asleep before nine o'clock last night. "I'll be there within the hour."

My idea of lounging about in the hotel's thick terry robe, followed by another decadent room-service order, went the way of all my other plans recently. I took a very quick shower and put on fresh clothes, then put the puppy in her crate and assured her I would be back soon.

The sun would peek over Sandia Crest in another few minutes, but already the day was beginning to press in with summer heat. I headed west to the police station and parked.

Gonzales came out for me within moments after I told the desk officer my name.

"Charlie. Good to see you looking so rested and refreshed."

I nodded at the tall, tan complected detective. The last time I'd seen him was during one of my debriefings, after four days on the run. He led the way down a couple of corridors and stopped at a door on the right.

"I remembered that you said the third man in the gang was named Ollie," he said. "Lucky I happened to be here when they brought this kid in. He was trying to break into the change machine at a coin laundry. His name is Oliver Trask."

Gonzales ushered me into the small room, which was lit only by a dim overhead fixture. Most of the light came from a window set in one wall, a two-way mirror that revealed an interrogation room.

The kid at the table was Ollie, all right. He looked thinner than I remembered and his blond hair lay in greasy strands. One end of his straggly mustache stuck out at a funny angle. He wore a T-shirt that said Jesus Loves You and didn't appear to have any socks on with his sneakers. Mainly, he looked alone and scared.

I nodded at Gonzales. "That's him."

"I'll turn on the sound," he said in a low voice. "You wait here. I'll go in there. So far, he's only been questioned about tonight's incident, with a few questions about where he was the day of the bank robbery. I want to see what else we can get out of him and then I'll check with you to see how much of his story is true."

He flipped a switch, picked up a can that I hadn't noticed on the console, and left the room. A second later, the door to the other room opened and Gonzales joined Ollie at the table.

"Hey, Ollie. Brought you a Coke." The cop set the can down in front of his suspect.

Ollie stared at the can but didn't pick it up. "When can I go home?"

"You don't have much experience at this do you, son? You're not going home right away. Even if we had all the answers we need from you, nobody's come to post your bond yet."

Ollie's gaze darted around the room as he performed some kind of mental Rolodex search for a name, someone who would come down here and get him out.

"You see, Ollie, there's more than just that half-assed attempt you made to get the money at the Laundromat. You've been identified as one of the men involved in a bank robbery/kidnapping last week."

I swore that Ollie's eyes fixed right on me.

Chapter 38

I stepped back from the glass, a little unnerved by the penetrating stare.

Gonzales slapped the table, snapping Ollie's attention back to the question at hand. "You haven't exactly come up with a very good explanation of where you were last Friday through Monday, and no one who can verify an alibi for you. So you see . . . we'll be needing to keep you here until we can do that."

"I told you, I borrowed a guy's car and drove to Texas. By myself."

"Yeah. Well, there is a motel clerk who remembers some of that. But he says you didn't even stay the night. You were there a few hours and then you left. Where'd you go after that?"

Ollie fidgeted in his chair. He picked up the open can of Coke and took a swallow but then he choked on it and sputtered a little.

Gonzales sat quietly, his eyes never leaving the young guy's face.

Ollie wiped his mouth on his shirt sleeve and shuffled in his seat some more. He couldn't seem to figure out what to do with his hands. He wanted so badly to look cool and in control but he just wasn't pulling it off.

Gonzales waited. I wondered if all interrogations involved this much silent staring. Finally, the cop gave a big sigh.

"Okay, Ollie, tell you what. There's a lot that we do know about that bank job. So maybe if I throw out a few details you can help fill in the blanks."

I could see the younger guy's wheels turning.

"We know the identities of two of your accomplices. Leon Mohler and Lonnie Stringer. They're guys with records, lot of unsavory stuff. Too bad they weren't put away sooner because this time they pulled a *really* bad one. Bank robbery and kidnapping are federal offenses. You know what that means? Longer prison terms, less likelihood of parole. Then there are the murders of Billy Hatchett, Melinda Davies and Sissy Davies."

Ollie gulped visibly when Gonzales mentioned the murders.

"For all we know, you might have been the guy who pulled the trigger on at least one of those murders."

Ollie's hands shook when he reached for the Coke can. He thought better of it and put the hands back in his lap.

Gonzales ran a hand over his shaved head. "You know, this state can't seem to figure out whether we want the death penalty or not. Sometimes it's in . . . sometimes it's out . . .. No telling which way it'll go by the time your case comes up."

The detective changed his tone, turning almost cheerful. "I'm gonna grab a cup of coffee. Want one? No? Okay, I'll be right back."

Ollie slumped in his chair the minute Gonzales was out the door. As the detective stepped into the room where I stood watching, Ollie began to weep quietly. He raked his fingers through his hair and pounded his forehead against the table.

"We'll let him stew for a few minutes. Hopefully, long enough to get him to turn on the others." He turned to me. "Is there anything you can think of that I can use as ammunition?"

I glanced back at Ollie. He'd never seemed like a hardened criminal to me, more like a kid who was desperately grasping for approval, anyone's approval.

"He told me that he was once pretty close to Sissy Davies. She wasn't technically related but he called her Aunt Sissy. Her death has to be weighing pretty heavily on him."

Gonzales nodded. "We didn't know about that yet."

"Billy's death might, too. I don't know. I didn't get a sense that they were close buddies, though. I think they only met recently. But String's shot, the one that killed Billy, it went right past Ollie's head. It shook him up."

"Good. I mean, that's helpful." Gonzales left again, was gone a few minutes and then entered the interrogation room with a cup of coffee in his hand.

"Okay, Ollie, where were we?" He stirred the coffee with one of those little wooden sticks and blew on the surface of the hot liquid. "Oh, yeah. Death penalty. Well, I'll tell you right now that we easily have enough evidence to put Stringer and Mohler away, and it's either going to be a life sentence or the death penalty. That's pretty much a sure thing."

He watched Ollie over the top of his cup as he took a sip.

"You and Billy Hatchett are equally culpable—that's means responsible—under the law because you were there. Just taking part in a crime where someone dies makes everyone guilty. Just in case you hadn't already learned from watching a lot of TV."

He took another slow sip, wasted another minute by staring into the cup, stirring it again with the little stick, blowing on the coffee. By this time Ollie was shifting in his seat like he was about to wet his pants.

"Only thing I need now is to get my hands on those other two. That's it." Gonzales sipped again. "We know they're back in the city. It's only a matter of time before they screw up and we catch 'em. And you know what—it'll be something stupid like the way we got you. Some dumb break-in for a few bucks."

Ollie's fingers drummed on the table now.

"See, the thing is—I'd really hate to see another innocent person get hurt when that happens. Because then it's the death penalty for sure. And I'm not so sure that we couldn't get your name tacked onto the list for that same sentence. Just depends on how good a lawyer you can afford." He chuckled. "Oh, I forgot. You didn't even have a quarter to your name. That's why you thought you had to knock over a laundry."

"I didn't do none of that shit," Ollie cried out. "I didn't go to that bank, I didn't shoot nobody, I didn't even get a share of the money." His voice cracked.

Gonzales let the words hang in the air for a minute. "Really? None of the bad stuff?" Another pause. "Well, then it's really a pisser that your name's going on that indictment. Well . . . unless . . ."

Ollie went for the bait. "Unless what? Maybe I can get some kind of a deal?"

"Well, I don't know. Like I said, we already got all the evidence we really need."

"You need to find them though," Ollie said. "I can help you."

Gonzales was as cool as I'd ever seen. He rubbed at his chin, while Ollie repeated the offer twice more.

"How're you going to do that?"

"I got to thinking," Ollie said, his voice as animated as one of the Little Rascals when they set out to make plans. "There's this house String owns. He doesn't always stay there. It's more like a safe house. Yeah, I think that's what he called it. His safe house."

"And you think he would go there now?"

"Yeah, sure. Makes sense, doesn't it? He said even his mother don't know about it."

"But you do. You know where it is."

"There was this one night when we was hiding out, at this farmhouse somewhere in Colorado . . . And String starts drinking and we's all playing cards and stuff. Right after he had the idea that the movie star lady would be worth a whole bunch of money. And Mole's asking him about how that would work, how we'd get the money and divvy it up."

Gonzales was writing notes on a yellow pad now.

"And String says that he'd meet the guy who's bringing the money and then we'd all meet up at String's house in Bernalillo and he'd give us each our share."

"But you were all headed to California together," Gonzales said. "So why come back to New Mexico to divide the money?"

"Oh, well String said it would be safer that way."

I sputtered out loud. How absolutely dumb could this guy be?

"Where in Bernalillo?" Gonzales asked.

"Huh?"

"Where is the house?"

I had to admire his ability to separate out the bullshit parts of the kid's story and stay with what he needed to know—where to find String now.

"He told Mole you take the main road into town, heading north. Two streets past this one Chevron station, fourth house on the left."

Gonzales asked a few more details but I lost track.

I, too, remembered something String said about having a safe house in Bernalillo. He'd hinted that the house was full of contraband.

Was Ollie setting us up?

Chapter 39

Gonzales came back into the observation room with me, while another officer cuffed Ollie and took him away.

"Finally," he said. "Looks like we might have a solid lead on a place to look. I'll get out there and check out that house."

"Dave, I don't know if that's a good idea," I said.

He gave me a quizzical look.

"When Ollie mentioned the house—well, I remembered a comment String made."

"And you didn't think to mention—"

"I know. I'm sorry. It just—"

"Tell me."

"As Ollie said, there was one night at the farmhouse when the men were drinking and playing cards. I had duct tape around my wrists and ankles and I was sitting in a corner of the kitchen, dozing about half the time, trying to plan a way out . . . Well, I didn't pay a lot of attention to the men. String tended to brag a lot—"

He twirled his hand in the air to make me hurry up.

"I think the house may be filled with weapons and explosives."

"What!"

"String did kind of mention a safe house. It came up while the guys were talking about the guns they'd used in the robbery, Mole admired one of the pistols . . . String said he had a place where he kept a whole lot more than those. Made it sound almost like an armory or something. Then he went off into bragging about how during his time in the Army he worked with C4 and a lot of explosives."

"Hmm . . . he might have. We do show that he did an Army stint in the mid-80s. I can check further on that."

"What I'm saying is that he's a really unbalanced dude. You can't believe the crazy—I'm talking insane—look he gets in his eyes. Dave, what if he was willing to blow the whole place up if your men cornered him there?"

"It could be a Waco-like scene, except that this place isn't out in the middle of nowhere. There are other houses all around."

I nodded. "Yeah."

He gripped the coffee cup that he'd carried in with him and stared at a spot in the middle of space.

"Okay, thanks. We'll have to figure out our best approach." He opened the door and held it for me.

"Wait. I have an idea," I said.

He paused, eyebrows raised.

"Let me be the bait and bring him out into the open, somewhere far away from his own turf."

"Absolutely not. No way. Forget it."

He was sounding a little too much like my husband now.

"Think about it, Dave. String has been sending me these notes, demanding money. The media said the robbers got away with fifty thousand dollars and he thinks I have it. I know, it's crazy. There was nowhere near that much and a lot of it was ruined by the dye . . . but he's got this idea that I can deliver a bunch of cash to him. What if we just played along with that?"

"I can't put a civilian at risk like this." He walked out into the corridor, headed toward the squad room.

I tagged along. "So, what . . . you'd tell him to meet up with a police officer and trust String to show up, just because he's fixated on the money? That's not exactly going to work."

Gonzales flopped into the chair at his desk, looking like he'd give anything to come up with a better idea so he could send me home.

"I'm not going to meet the guy in some dark alley. We'd choose a place that's nice and open. You'd set your men up in advance to grab them. I'll wear a vest and carry a weapon."

"No. More civilians get hurt when they brandish a weapon at a criminal than you'd like to believe."

I had a feeling this might become our sticking point, so I just kept my mouth shut.

He tapped a pen against the yellow pad that contained his notes from the interview with Ollie. I could see his wheels turning.

"Let's say that I did agree with this plan. And let's say that we could find a good spot to do it, where we control the action. How would we contact Stringer and Mohler and get them to come?"

I sat in the visitor chair beside the desk. I hadn't gotten quite this far in the plan.

"I would have to talk to him."

"I don't like it."

Truthfully, I didn't like it much either once I thought about it. I tapped a fingernail on the desktop as I considered what to do.

"Okay, how about this? He found my office and confronted me there once. Then he left two notes. He'll come back." I outlined the rest of the steps, basically, as I thought them up.

Chapter 40

From the bay window in my darkened office I scoped out the street below. Streetlamps illuminated the pre-dawn neighborhood where nothing had moved since I arrived thirty minutes ago. The two government vehicles had not been back since yesterday, although their earlier presence had not exactly deterred String from approaching the building with his most recent note.

"Clear in the back," Ron called out. "We better get moving."

I grabbed up the note I'd written earlier, telling String that I had the money and wanted to meet. We made our way down the stairs, leaving the normal daytime lights on throughout the offices. Ron peeked through the curtains at the back window, re-checking the parking area, before giving me the go-ahead. We locked the door and stuck the note in the jamb, then hurried to his car. I ducked into the back seat and stayed low, while he pulled out. My Jeep stayed behind.

Everything about the place was meant to look as if I were working here alone. Now all I had to do was stay somewhere out of sight until String found the note and called the phone number I'd written there. It went to a cell phone that APD gave me, one they could easily monitor.

Ron drove through the semi-residential neighborhood of our office at his normal pace and then told me I could raise up once we got to the busier streets beyond. Within fifteen minutes he'd delivered me to my uptown hotel, where Drake and Freckles had just come in from her morning walk.

"Did you leave the note on the door at home?" I asked.

"Yep, as ordered." Drake pulled me into his arms but I found it hard to relax into the embrace as I normally love to do.

"I feel jumpy as a cat," I said. "Until we hear something . . . no, make that until those two are locked away."

"I know," he said. "We'll all be relieved when this is over."

Poor thing. He's put up with a lot of drama in my life. I would have to think of a suitable thank-you that I could offer for his tolerance of the whole situation. From the way his hands were wandering I got the idea that he already had a reward in mind. Of course, his wandering hands led me to think of places to put my own hands . . .

And then the special cell phone rang.

We jumped apart as if we'd been hit by a jolt of electricity. My hands shook as I flipped it open and pressed the Talk button.

"Don't worry, it's just me," said Detective Gonzales. "Everything in place?"

Yeah, except my stomach. I willed it to stop doing flips and assured him that the first part of the plan had gone perfectly. We went over the instructions I was to give to String when he called. I'd even written them down in case I was too fuzzled to remember them exactly when the phone call came.

"Now we wait," Gonzales said before he hung up.

Yes, waiting was the only choice. Unfortunately, the romantic mood had vanished now that I had some time with nothing to do. Drake suggested a big room-service breakfast and I left him to make the choices and place the call while I took a shower.

Passing time before an unpleasant event has never been a strong suit of mine. I would always rather anticipate Christmas morning than a trip to the dentist, for instance. We'd agreed that we would both stay inside the room, mainly to avoid the complications that would happen if one of us were away when the call came. Drake still didn't want me taking the risk of running into String accidentally either. Another kidnapping was off our to-do list for a good long time now.

Drake spent part of the morning on his own phone, touching base with clients and making plans for some upcoming jobs with the helicopter. I attempted to read a book but actually read one sentence about three hundred times before I finally gave up and began pacing the floor.

It was nearly four o'clock when the special cell phone rang again. This time I recognized the number on the readout as Dave Gonzales's.

"No word yet?" he asked. "We've had men watching the house in Bernalillo since last night. No sign of Stringer or Mohler all day."

Unfortunately, I couldn't give him any good news.

"Remember, when you hear from them, to allow at least an hour before the meeting. My men will try to track them but it won't be a sure thing. We may not know how close they are at the time they call you."

I had just ended the call when a knock at our hotel room door sent the dog into a barking frenzy and my heart rate into the stratosphere. Drake pulled his pistol and approached the door quietly, checking through the peephole before relaxing and admitting Ron.

"Hey," my brother said. "I'm done with other stuff for the day. Any word?"

I filled him in on the late-breaking news.

The next hour went by, as Elsa would say, slower than molasses in January. I alternated between wishing the crooks would just hurry up and call and hoping they'd forgotten all about the money. I didn't get lucky on either version of the wish.

The red numerals on the clock had just clicked to 6:00 when the call came. The readout only said "unknown." My voice seemed very tentative when I said hello.

"Hello, Charlie." String's oily voice brought back all the horror. "So you *did* get the money for me."

"I've got it right here." I eyed the large black duffle on the floor. It contained a layer of banded bills, on top of a thick stack of blank paper. If it had all been the real thing that would have provided another tempting reason for me to abandon this whole crazy scheme and take off for Barbados. But I wouldn't have done that. They have an extradition agreement.

"Bring it to—"

"No, String. This time I'm saying how it goes. You need this bag more than I need anything at all from you."

Tough talk that I could not possibly enforce.

He growled something about not being so sure about that.

"Seven-thirty. The parking lot of the shopping center at Juan Tabo and Montgomery. I'll drive up in a silver pickup truck. I want to see both you and Mole."

"I'm coming by myself."

This was the one contingency that none of us could guarantee and Gonzales had left it up to me to make a convincing argument why both men should be there.

"Hunh-uh. No way am I going to let him sneak up behind me while I'm talking face-to-face with you. You two drive up together and I better not see a weapon on either of you. Once I see you both, I'll set the money bag on the ground and then get in my vehicle and leave." I clicked off the call before he had a chance to respond.

It was chancy, I knew, but better than getting into a discussion and giving him the chance to make an alternate suggestion. This whole deal had to be on my terms.

Chapter 41

Immediately, I called Gonzales and let him know that we were leaving. Drake helped me get rigged up with the wire that Gonzales had insisted I wear. He clipped the battery pack to the waistband of my shorts, ran the microphone wire under my cotton shirt and handed me the receiver piece which I plugged into my ear. At the time, I'd scoffed at the idea, but now I was glad for the contact.

From our uptown hotel I was less than fifteen minutes to the drop site. If String and Mole were still down in the valley, anywhere near my office, they were at least thirty or forty-five minutes away. If they'd somehow divined that they would be going to the far northeast heights, well, that might be a problem. They could get there ahead of me.

At least they wouldn't get there ahead of the police.

We put Freckles into her crate and stocked her up with a few treats, which she gobbled before I'd hardly closed the door. Drake would ride with Ron in his car and I took the keys to Drake's pickup truck. They stayed a few car lengths behind me as we headed northeast through the city. I approached the chosen intersection and pulled in, taking in the neat tan stucco buildings with their green trim and awnings.

Gonzales had assured me that his people were in place but I sure didn't spot them. The small center contained a number of neighborhood businesses plus a good-sized bookstore. People were moving about, although I hoped the fact that the meeting was taking place at the dinner hour would mean that the place wouldn't be crowded. If things got ugly . . . well, it didn't bear thinking about at this point. We were committed.

I pulled into a parking slot at the corner of the lot farthest from all the businesses. Ron found a spot about three rows away, facing his car toward me. Reassuring to see both of their faces watching me. Scary that I was about to be facing down the two men who'd killed three other people in their lust for this money.

The sun was blasting in through the west-facing side of the truck, low in the sky. It would be down soon and I hoped that the whole business of catching the crooks would be over with before dark. I felt apprehensive and yet buoyed at the prospect of an end to this whole thing.

People came and went. Mothers with kids in their cars pulled into the drive-thru lanes of a fast food place on the opposite corner. A white-haired man came out of the electronics store with a small bag in his hand. A man with longish hair, wearing shorts and a T-shirt stood outside the bookstore, leaning on a post and reading a newspaper. He might be one of the cops.

I tested my microphone by sending out a call for Dave Gonzales. No response. That didn't help my jittery stomach at all.

Ten minutes ticked by. The miniscule earpiece that Drake had hidden under my hair sizzled with static.

"Detective Gonzales? Are you there?"

"Roger that, Charlie. I'm at your nine o'clock."

I glanced beyond my left shoulder and spotted him in a plain car. He didn't look my direction or acknowledge me.

"Our men caught sight of them about a block away," he said. "They're driving a green Cadillac. Keep watching— okay, there it is."

If I thought I had a nervous stomach before . . . now it did a few gymnastic moves.

"Stay cool, Charlie. He's coming up on your four o'clock. He'll be . . ." His voice trailed off as the Cadillac came into my view.

I reassured myself that my pistol was under the seat of the truck. Drake insisted that I have it with me. Gonzales was equally adamant that I not carry it on my person. Spotting it would be the kind of thing that could set String off. If that were to happen anyway, my plan was to dash for the truck, get behind the door and have a hand on my weapon.

The green car slowly cruised up the aisle in front of the buildings. String and Mole were in the front seats, their heads turning, scanning for signs of trouble. They made a wide circle and came around to face me.

"Get out, Charlie, and set the bag down. You don't want them coming in close to your vehicle," Gonzales said into my ear.

Showtime. I grabbed the bag and lugged it across the

seats as I stepped out. The green car was a hundred yards away.

I speed-walked to an open spot twenty yards from the truck. Took a deep breath and set the bag down.

The green car moved forward slowly.

I backed away, holding my arms out to my sides, palms up.

In my ear, I could hear Gonzales rapping out orders to his men but I couldn't make out what he was saying. All at once his voice came clearly into my ear again. "Charlie, get back to your truck now!"

I quickened my pace, backing toward the truck but keeping the green car in sight. String must have picked up on my nervousness. He gunned the car and came straight at me.

Chapter 42

So much for taking cover behind the door of the truck. I immediately figured out that if the Cadillac hit the truck, I'd be squash. I sprinted for the edge of the parking lot where curbing bordered a narrow band of landscaping. Somehow I hoped that the overgrown shrubs and the lone sycamore tree would protect me.

String roared up beside the bag of money, and Mole opened his door and made a grab for the handles on the duffle.

"They're taking the money!" I shouted to the world at large.

Gonzales and his team, however, had already spotted String's maneuver. The whole parking lot instantly went into motion.

A brown van zipped to within inches of the passenger side of Drake's truck, forming an effective blockade to

String's escape to the west. Gonzales himself did a similar move on the east side. An APD cruiser roared in behind the Caddy—where had he come from?—and a female officer dressed in casual summer wear emerged from a parked car, whipped out her service pistol and screamed at the two crooks to freeze.

Mole lost his grasp on the money bag. He tried to pull his door shut but centrifugal force swung it even farther open. One of the officers had him out by the collar and facedown on the pavement before he knew what hit him. String attempted to steer the car with one hand; the other came up with a pistol. Incongruously, I noticed that his hands were still bright pink from the bank dye. Gonzales had a two-handed grip on his own weapon and it was trained firmly on String's face.

"Drop it!" he screamed. The intensity of his expression left no doubt that he would fire first and answer questions later.

Way to go, Dave!

String let his pistol fall to the seat, and the Caddy came to a slow rolling stop against the bumper of Drake's truck.

I realized that I was standing knee deep in a massive clump of pampas grass whose whip-like strands were trying to slice my bare legs to ribbons. My hands were over my mouth and my eyes must have been about the size of dinner plates.

Handcuffs snapped onto the two felons so quickly that I nearly missed it in a blink. The killers were lying face-down on the ground and the whole scene began to draw a little crowd. Dave Gonzales picked up the duffle full of money and quickly locked it into the trunk of his vehicle before anyone could take advantage of it.

String's baleful glare followed the movements of the bag. Then he turned that stare on me.

Yikes. I really hoped Gonzales had been right about these guys getting maximum sentences.

Chapter 43

That edgy feeling waxed and waned over the coming weeks as the whole bank robbery and kidnapping were relived in the media. Once they knew my real identity, the media swarmed me for awhile. Well, okay, it was only about two days—some ill-timed earthquake in Chile took away my steam pretty fast.

I couldn't forget the hatred in String's eyes as the police pulled him up off the asphalt and shoved him into the backseat of a cruiser. It seemed that he'd fixed all the blame for his lost riches upon me. Because I wasn't really Cristina Cross? Because I'd tricked him to that parking lot on that particular evening? I had no idea.

When I saw the newspaper announcement of Billy's funeral I called his mother. She was clearly in shock, with no understanding of how her son became involved. I couldn't offer any answers to that, but I did my best to let her know that he'd been pretty decent to me. Grabbing me in the bank and tying me up had clearly been done under String's orders, after all. By the time the call ended, neither of us really felt a lot better but I'd done my best.

I found myself being extra careful about locking doors and windows for weeks, until I realized that the trials would still be months away and I wasn't doing myself any good by stressing over it constantly.

Gradually, life at home and at the office has returned to normal. Ron and Victoria are looking pretty serious and I keep speculating about whether there might be an autumn wedding in the family. She would be a fun sister-in-law, somebody who would get me out of the office once in awhile. She might even instill some fashion sense into me.

Our other new family member is fitting right in. Freckles has become quite the watchdog and very protective of me, and it's largely because of her that I've relaxed somewhat. Maybe that early imprinting, the day Drake found her during the time he'd been so worried for my safety caused her to bond to me. Her unconditional love fills my heart, and I'm glad we share our lives with her.

**Books
by Connie Shelton**

THE CHARLIE PARKER SERIES

Deadly Gamble
Vacations Can Be Murder
Partnerships Can Be Murder
Small Towns Can Be Murder
Memories Can Be Murder
Honeymoons Can Be Murder
Reunions Can Be Murder
Competition Can Be Murder
Balloons Can Be Murder
Obsessions Can Be Murder
Gossip Can Be Murder
Stardom Can Be Murder

Holidays Can Be Murder - a Christmas novella

THE SAMANTHA SWEET SERIES

Sweet Masterpiece
Sweet's Sweets

What's Next?

Yes, there will be another new Charlie Parker mystery in 2012. Visit our website and sign up for Connie's free email mystery newsletter so you'll be among the first to receive the announcement.

Connie is pleased to introduce a new mystery series, featuring Samantha Sweet.
Sam breaks into houses for a living.
But she's really a baker with a magical touch, who invites you to her delightful pastry shop—
Sweet's Sweets.
There's a little mystery, a little romance, and a touch of the paranormal.
Don't miss the all of the fun books in this series!

Sign up for Connie's free email mystery newsletter for announcements of new books, discount coupons, and the chance to win some terrific prizes.

www.connieshelton.com